"I shouldn't have kissed you."

Holt's black eyes hardened as he continued. "If you'd been a man, I'd have knocked you on your backside. But since you aren't a man…"

"You kissed me." The sooner they faced facts, the sooner… what? Did they pretend the kiss never happened? It would take a heap of pretending, that was for darn sure.

"It won't happen again," he stated baldly. "I don't kiss my employees, nor do I kiss city slickers. And you qualify on both counts."

"I may be your employee, but I'm no—" Cami broke off at the look on his face. "What's wrong with kissing city slickers?"

For a moment, she didn't think he'd answer. "Last time I kissed one, I ended up married to her. That mistake almost lost me my ranch."

Dear Reader,

As children we've all dreamed of what we'd be when we grew up, and for many, being a cowboy was a cherished dream. It certainly was for me.

I've long believed that a cowboy isn't just a person, but a way of life. A state of mind. My image of a cowboy has always been that of a loner with a strong code of ethics, someone who faces adversity head-on, someone who'd sooner die than betray his honor. I fell in love with that image.

But childhood dreams have a tendency to fall by the wayside as we mature. We realize that being a cowboy isn't practical, so we leave behind those summer days when we were Billy the Kid or Marshall Dillon or joined Wyatt Earp as he faced down the Clantons. We hang up our six-shooter and our ten-gallon hat and turn our attention to more realistic pursuits. But we still smile reminiscently when we watch a Western, and a part of us longs to taste, just once, the thrill of being a cowboy.

I guess that's why I wrote *Once a Cowboy....* So for all of you who, as children, stood in a dusty street at high noon to prove you were the fastest draw in the West, I give you Cami Greenbush, someone who never gave up her dream to be an honest-to-goodness cowboy.

Sincerely,

Day Leclaire

ONCE A COWBOY...
Day Leclaire

Harlequin Books

TORONTO • NEW YORK • LONDON
AMSTERDAM • PARIS • SYDNEY • HAMBURG
STOCKHOLM • ATHENS • TOKYO • MILAN
MADRID • WARSAW • BUDAPEST • AUCKLAND

To our family's own "Marlboro Man,"
my father, Stephen M. Totton,
who first introduced me to
the wonders of the West

ISBN 0-373-03301-X

ONCE A COWBOY...

Copyright © 1994 by Day Leclaire.

All rights reserved. Except for use in any review, the reproduction or
utilization of this work in whole or in part in any form by any electronic,
mechanical or other means, now known or hereafter invented, including
xerography, photocopying and recording, or in any information storage
or retrieval system, is forbidden without the written permission of the
publisher, Harlequin Enterprises Limited, 225 Duncan Mill Road,
Don Mills, Ontario, Canada M3B 3K9.

All characters in this book have no existence outside the imagination of
the author and have no relation whatsoever to anyone bearing the same
name or names. They are not even distantly inspired by any individual
known or unknown to the author, and all incidents are pure invention.

This edition published by arrangement with Harlequin Enterprises B. V.

® and TM are trademarks of the publisher. Trademarks indicated with
® are registered in the United States Patent and Trademark Office, the
Canadian Trade Marks Office and in other countries.

Printed in U.S.A.

PROLOGUE

At the A-OK Corral,
outside Lullabye, Colorado...

HOLT WINSTON flipped through the stack of resumés cluttering his desk, his expression growing darker by the minute. Dammit! Why had he waited so long to fill the last remaining wrangler position? Procrastination wasn't his usual style. But it sure had grabbed hold on this particular task.

He glanced at the next resumé and tossed it impatiently to one side. He knew damned well why he sat here as stubborn as a mule asked to jump the Grand Canyon. It was for one reason and one reason only.

Hiring hands for a *dude* ranch gnawed at him, twisting in his gut like a blunt-edged knife.

Being good with rope, horse and cow wasn't enough any more. To be worth their salt, wranglers who worked dude ranches had to be good with people, too. A sorry state of affairs, that's what it was. But one he'd put up with until he'd got himself back in the black. And the only way to do *that* was to open his gates to outsiders.

Now because of his little... aversion, all the good wranglers were taken. Which left him a day late, a dollar short, a man shy and knee-deep in cow— Hold the horses!

He snatched a resumé from the pile and tipped back his hat. Well, now. If that didn't beat all. Here in the middle of this heap of manure, he'd found a gold nugget. A gold nugget by the name of Tex Greenbush. A natural-born cowboy who, if the people recommending him weren't exaggerating, could "sweet-talk the rattle off a diamondback."

Considering the strange and varied "city slickers" who visited each year, a sweet-talking wrangler was one he couldn't afford to pass up. Hell, he couldn't afford to pass up a wrangler who could string more than two words together.

That decided, he yanked his standard contract from a drawer, scrawled his signature on the bottom and stuffed it into an envelope with a brief acceptance note. A lick and a stamp and it was ready for the post office. With a practiced snap of his fingers, he sent the envelope spinning lazily through the air. It landed smack-dab in the center of the "outgoing" box on the far edge of his desk.

Then he tilted his oak swivel chair to a reckless angle and lifted a mud-spattered boot, dropping it square on top of the remaining resumés. Settling his hat low over his eyes, he grabbed his chipped mug and took a deep, satisfying swallow of coffee as thick as molasses and black as tar. Yep. Now that that minor detail was taken care of, he could enjoy the rest of his day.

Life was perfect.

*A few days later
in Richmond, Virginia...*

CAMI GREENBUSH whooped for joy. "I did it! Holy mackerel, he hired me!" Tossing the letter, envelope and contract she'd received into the air, she rushed to the window and flung it open, leaning out farther than caution dictated. "Hey, everybody!" she shouted, thick black curls tumbling about her flushed face. "I'm not just a cowboy, any more. I'm Tex Greenbush. A gen-u-ine, hired-for-the-season, *employed* cowboy!"

Enthusiastic applause greeted her announcement. "Way to go, Cami!" one neighbor yelled.

"We knew you could do it!"

"That's our girl!"

She beamed at the well-wishers. "This calls for one heck of a celebration. Texas style, of course. You're all invited. Tonight. Up here. Seven o'clock. And fair warning, the chili's gonna be tongue-blisterin' hot!"

"Er, Cami," her roommate, Diane, interrupted. "Have you read this acceptance letter?"

Cami retreated from her precarious position at the window. "Sure I have. It said, 'You're hired.' What else is there to read?"

Diane sighed, studying the papers. "Well, the contract for one thing. It stipulates a two-week trial period."

"No problem."

"No problem, unless this Holt Winston decides you can't do the job. Then, according to this, he can fire you."

"He won't," Cami reassured Diane blithely, crossing to the kitchen. "Did I buy extra chili peppers last time I went shopping? I'm sure I did... We'll need lots for tonight."

Diane trailed after her. "Cami! Will you pay attention? Once Mr. Winston realizes you can't rope, haven't been near a ranch in more than twenty years and the last horse you rode was connected to a carousel, he'll have you on the next plane out of there.''

Cami poked through the refrigerator. ''Train. Real cowboys use two and only two forms of transportation. Their horse. And, when they absolutely must, a train.''

''*Cami!*''

''What?''

''He's going to discover you lied on that resumé and that's going to make him very angry.''

Cami rocked back on her heels and glared indignantly at her roommate. ''Lied? What lies are you talking about?''

''Your roping skills for one,'' Diane said pointedly.

''Oh, that.'' Cami shrugged. ''Everyone knows Texans are prone to exaggeration. I admit, one or two details might be open to broad interpretation. But I wouldn't call them lies. Lying is wrong. And if there's one thing I never am, it's wrong.''

Irony tinged Diane's voice. ''There's another thing you're not, and that's a wrangler.''

''Sure I am. I just need practice.''

''You need to have your head examined.''

Cami returned her attention to her pepper search. ''You don't understand.''

''What don't I understand?'' her roommate asked in exasperation.

''That I'm a Texan. Which means I'm a cowboy by birth. The rest will come naturally.''

Diane groaned. ''You've got to be kidding.''

''It's not a problem,'' Cami insisted. ''You'll see. Cowboying is in my genes.'' With a smothered exclamation, she grabbed a plastic bag half-hidden behind a carton of milk. ''Found you, you devils.'' She held the chili peppers aloft and grinned in triumph.

Life was perfect.

CHAPTER ONE

WES SLOWED HIS BATTERED pickup and made a sharp right, bouncing onto a long dirt road. "Here we are," he said to Cami. "Around this next bend is the A-OK Corral."

Cami scooted to the edge of her seat and strained for her first glimpse of the place she'd call home for the next several months. The truck cleared a rise and a huge ranch appeared before her. She sighed in delight. It was the embodiment of a lifelong fantasy and perfect in every detail.

The builder had tucked the two-story log house into a hillside. Behind it the Rocky Mountains rose sharply, stabbing the intense blue sky with craggy, snowcapped peaks. A stand of ponderosa pine surrounded the buildings and a sweep of green daisy-studded scrub grass bobbed beneath the late spring breeze like a living welcome mat.

Off to the right of the main house and dotted amongst the trees were several smaller cabins. For the help, she wondered, or the guests? To the left stood the barn and corral. A meadowlark called to her from the fence post, it's flutelike song a pleasant welcome. She inhaled deeply, taking in the brisk mountain air. What could be more ideal than this?

She turned to Wes. "Thanks for the lift," she said with a wide grin. "And tell that wife of yours to visit real soon."

"You can count on it. Remember, you promised to come by my shop for a soda next time you're in Lullabye."

Cami ticked off on her fingers: "And by Clara's for more cowboy duds—she dressed me up real fine, didn't she? And by Reverend Sam's for a chat—Lordy, that man can chat. And by Trudy's Feminine Fripperies for any unmentionables I might need—though what half that stuff is, is beyond me." She caught her breath before adding, "Oh, yeah. And by Lem's Mercantile and General Gathering Spot for—well, just for the heck of it, I guess. That sure is one friendly town you have there. Who's left to meet?"

Wes thought a minute. "You missed Tommy Torrino. But he's down Denver way and won't return till tomorrow. He's our mayor."

Cami grimaced. "I guess that's what I get coming in a day early."

Wes climbed out of his pickup and plucked her suitcase from the bed of his truck. "That's youth. Always in a hurry to be gettin' and doin'. Guess I'll shove off, if you're positive you'll be okay."

"Not just okay. Being back on a ranch..." She blinked away an unexpected tear, her smile wobbling a bit. "I've dreamed about it for a long time. I can't believe I'm finally here."

"Now, now." He patted her shoulder. "You need anything, anything a'tall, you give me or Sadie a holler."

Impulsively, Cami threw her arms around him. "Thanks, Wes."

He gave her an awkward hug, than scrambled into his truck. "Tell Holt howdy. And don't be a stranger, hear?"

"Will do."

Wes started his engine and reversed out of the yard in a huge plume of dust. Cami waved, then turned and crossed to the ranch house. It seemed unnaturally silent. To be on the safe side, she banged on the front door. No one answered. Maybe arriving ahead of schedule hadn't been the smartest idea, after all.

Nonsense! she scolded. It showed incentive. It showed drive. It showed an eagerness to start work. Who wouldn't appreciate that? She'd tuck away her suitcase on this fine porch of Mr. Winston's and borrow his equally fine rocker. Eventually someone would show up to welcome her, and they'd be delighted she'd had the good sense to come early. In the meantime, she'd relax and enjoy the view.

She'd no sooner settled herself in the rocker than an approaching cloud of dust heralded the arrival of another vehicle. A few minutes later, a station wagon pulled into the yard and a man in his late thirties climbed from behind the wheel, looking around in bewilderment. He poked his head in the open car window and said something to the woman seated on the passenger side. In the back, Cami could see several wriggling children. The family's youngest member announced his presence with a strident wail.

Cami glanced from the silent ranch house to the car. This wasn't right. These were guests, no doubt about it. Someone should be here to meet them. It wouldn't do for their introduction to the A-OK Corral to be so lacking in welcome. Coming to a swift decision, she stood, hitched up her britches and strode across to the car.

"Howdy!" she shouted over the shrieks of their baby. "Cami Greenbush at your service." She stuck out her hand.

The man latched onto it in relief. "Rob Radburn," he said, pumping her arm up and down. "I didn't think we'd ever get here. We've been on the road for four days straight, and the kids..." He turned a harassed gaze toward the car. "They're sort of sick of being penned up in there."

"Completely understandable." Gingerly, Cami eased her crimped fingers from his desperate grip and peered in the car. The woman on the passenger side stared blankly out the front windshield. "Er, your wife?"

A young freckle-faced redhead popped from the rear of the station wagon. "Aw, she's been like that for the last day and a half. Randy was foolin' around with his slingshot and it sort of went off by itself and beaned her one."

Rob shuffled in the dust. "It was supposed to be a second honeymoon," he mumbled. "But Rhonda and I couldn't find anyone to take the kids."

"Well, they'll have plenty of running space here." Cami leaned in the rear car door and hauled out the nearest squirming body. "So. Where do you all hail from?"

"Ohio. Columbus, to be exact."

"You don't say. Well, don't worry." She winked broadly. "I won't hold it against you, even though I'm a Texan myself."

He managed a weak grin. "Thanks. This is sort of new to us," he admitted, clearly at a loss. "What... what should I be doing?"

"Unloading sounds good to me. I'll start with these fellas, if you'll unhook that roof rack." She caught the belt of the next youngster and yanked him into the sunshine. Two bodies later, she came across the noisy one. "Hey, I think this little guy's hungry. Is there a bottle handy?"

With a grunt, Rob unlatched the roof rack and struggled to free the first suitcase. "Try the cooler."

Within minutes she had the baby freed from his car seat, a bottle in his mouth and peace restored. Next, she turned her attention to the assorted redheads wrestling in the dirt. "Okay, boys. Everybody grab a bag or suitcase and carry it to the porch. Once that's done, I'll show you some of the best yo-yo tricks this side of the Mississippi."

It took a bit of work, but she soon had them organized. She even managed to cajole Rhonda from the car, onto the porch and into the rocker.

"Sit down anywhere. Make yourself comfortable." Cami reached in the pocket of her brand spanking new jeans and tugged out a yo-yo. "Rory, the baby doesn't eat lizards. Give it up. And Rufus, you shake that can of soda one more time and you won't get to try my buckin' bronco trick. Now, come stand by me and watch how it's done."

She grinned at her obedient audience. Hey, this was a snap. She was really getting the hang of this cowboying stuff!

"I DO BELIEVE WE'VE GOT company, Holt," Gabby announced, reining in his mount beside Holt and Frank. "You expectin' anybody?"

Holt swiveled in the saddle and stared at his ranch house through narrowed eyes. "Only that new wrangler, Tex Greenbush. But he's not due till tomorrow. Whoever they are, they've made a mistake."

The old-timer snorted. "Looks to me like that mistake's taken over your entire front porch."

Holt glanced at his neighbor. "They yours, Frank?"

"Could be," he admitted with a shrug. "I have a passel of Radburns arriving anytime now. I suppose that could be them. Wonder why Miss Agnes hasn't sent them on their way?"

"She's on vacation," Holt said. "Not due back until next week." He examined the group.

They weren't local, that was for damned sure. Even from this distance he could make out the standard uniform of a tourist—plaid shorts, T-shirt, white socks and sneakers, and the mandatory camera strung around the neck. Most striking of all was the expanse of pale skin, which at this altitude, near guaranteed a nasty sunburn.

"It would appear I've been overrun by a herd of redheads—a herd of redheads with a mountain of luggage."

Gabby yanked on his mustache. "Except for the one in the cowboy hat. He's no redhead."

"If your eyes weren't as ancient as the rest of you," Holt informed him drily, "you'd see he's a female."

"And a fine-figured one at that," Frank added. He leaned forward and squinted into the sun. "Getting old sure is hell. I can't quite see what she's playing with. Some kind of ball?"

"Nope. A yo-yo."

Gabby peered down the mountainside. "Get on with you! A yo-yo? I never heard such a ridiculous—"

"You'll see soon enough." Holt circled his horse around a pile of boulders. "Come on. Let's get this settled and those folks on their way. We've got fences to mend." He nudged Loco into a trot and started down the hill, Gabby and Frank at his heels.

Pulling up alongside the porch, he eyed the group and buried a smile. Yep. Tourists. He tugged at the brim of his hat. "Excuse me," he said. "Mind if I ask what's going on here?"

The yo-yo whistled past the kids, coming to within a hair of Holt's nose, froze in midair, then snapped back into the woman's hands. In one smooth move it disappeared into the pocket of a heavily starched pair of jeans.

She turned to face him, a wide, appealing grin splitting her face. "Hey, there," she called in greeting. She trotted across the wooden planks of the porch, her gait a bit stiff legged from the bat-wing leather chaps she wore, and on down the stairs, huge, pointy spurs jangling with every step.

She was a looker, no two ways about it—for a city slicker. He struggled to keep a straight face, trying to ignore her pseudo-western gear. But it was tough ignoring a loud red, white and blue checked shirt with silly silver fringe dangling from every conceivable seam. It was even tougher to ignore her longhorn-cow buckle—a buckle that threatened to gore anybody who came within courtin' distance. But it was toughest of all to ignore the perfectly good Stetson perched atop her head. A Stetson that some fool had dyed pink and decorated with more feathers than a gaggle of geese. One good gust and she'd be airborne.

"Been shopping at Clara's?" Holt couldn't resist asking. Beside him, Frank choked. Gabby proceeded to thump their neighbor on the back. Hard.

Eyes as wide and blue as the morning sky stared up at Holt from beneath a tumble of thick, curly black hair. "Clara did me up real fine, didn't she?"

He swallowed his laughter, the ingenuousness of her expression stealing the urge to tease clean away. "She aims to satisfy," he conceded gruffly.

As though remembering her manners, she doffed her hat. Feathers spurted into the air, drifting downward to snag in her hair and in the fringe of her shirt. "How do?" she said. "Cami Greenbush at your service. I work for Mr. Holt Winston and since he's not around, I thought I'd help his guests unload and keep them entertained." She gestured toward the porch. "This is Rob and Rhonda Radburn and their boys, Randy, Rory, Rufus, Rollie, Rusty and—" She glanced uncertainly at the baby.

"Junior," Rob supplied.

Cami grinned. "And Junior."

Holt tensed, mild amusement rapidly dissipating as a horrible suspicion grabbed hold. A suspicion he sincerely hoped would prove wrong. "Did you say your name is *Greenbush?*" he bit out, praying for once his ears had deceived him.

"I surely did. Actually, it's Camellia Greenbush," she admitted.

"Camellia..."

She scowled. "God's honest truth. I'm a Texan, myself. But my momma is from Virginia and thought it would be kinda cute to name me after her favorite shrub."

"Camellia..."

"Now, don't rub it in. With the last name Greenbush, nobody would want to lug around a handle like Camellia. Leastwise, I wouldn't. But I don't hold it against Momma. She meant well...I guess. Still, I'd appreciate it if you'd call me Cami. Okay?''

For a split second there was stunned silence. Then Frank exploded with laughter, Gabby muttered a colorful expletive and Holt closed his eyes. No way. If there was an ounce of fairness in the world, it wouldn't be true. But how many Greenbushes could one planet hold? The odds of this one being anybody other than the wrangler he'd hired were staggering.

He fixed her with a stern gaze. "First, Holt Winston's around now. You're conversing with him. Second, these aren't my guests. They belong to my neighbor here, Frank Smith."

Frank, still fighting to bring his amusement under control, flicked the brim of his hat with his forefinger. "Ma'am," he said.

"And third," Holt continued in a hard voice. "I don't have an employee named Cami Greenbush."

Not one whit abashed, that stunning smile reappeared, along with two deep dimples in her cheeks. "True enough. But you do have an employee named Tex Greenbush and they're both me." She offered her hand. "Pleased to meet you, Mr. Winston."

"Likewise, I'm sure. You're fired."

Her hand dropped slowly to her side, her smile faltering. "Fired?"

"Fired. I hired an experienced wrangler, not a duded-up schoolgirl."

She planted her hands on her hips and stuck her chin into the air, a flush blooming across her cheekbones. Holt released his breath in a silent sigh. He'd had close and personal experience with other females wearing that particular expression. Unfortunately, it usually meant the wearer intended to tear a strip off his hide with the cutting edge of her tongue.

"You can't fire me," she announced. "We've got a contract."

He nodded. "And I just broke it."

To his amazement, the light of battle faded and she burst out laughing. He shot a look at Gabby and Frank, relieved to see he wasn't the only one she'd taken by surprise. Their jaws hung somewhere in the vicinity of their belt buckles.

"You figure she got hold of some locoweed?" Gabby asked in a loud aside, scratching his whiskered jaw in puzzlement.

Holt didn't respond. Instead he leaned across his saddle horn and waited, waited until her laughter died and those incredible blue eyes were once again fixed squarely on his. Then he spoke in his most cordial—and most discouraging—tone of voice. The voice smart people took heed of. The one that kept even the more ornery of his wranglers toeing the line.

The one he used right before he decked someone.

"Something...amusin' you, miss?" he asked softly.

She didn't appear in the least intimidated, let alone as scared as any soul in her proper mind ought to be. He watched in stunned disbelief as she stepped within reach of him and ran a gentle hand along Loco's neck. To his utter disgust, the dumb horse stood there and took it.

"It's just...I know a cowboy's word means more than that. We have a contract. You'd sooner shoot yourself in the foot than go back on your word." She peered at him from beneath ridiculously long, thick lashes. "Isn't that right?"

His brows snapped together. "Where the hell did you get such a harebrained notion as—"

"Er, Holt?"

He turned and glared at his foreman. "What?"

Gabby gave a significant nod toward the porch. "You was sayin'?"

Holt glanced at the litter of pitcher-eared redheads lining his railing. Sixteen narrowed, unblinking eyes appraised him with cold disapproval. "I was saying...I...You..." He fought hard to rein in the words clamoring to be spoken. Jamming his Stetson low on his brow, he gritted his teeth. *Blasted female.* "I was saying, gol'durn it, that of course a cowboy always keeps his word."

She beamed. There was no other word for it. Even the smattering of freckles across her pert upturned nose glowed. "I knew it! A cowboy, a *real* cowboy is always true to his horse, true to his woman and true to his word."

Gabby slapped a gloved hand to his chest. "God bless America!" he exclaimed.

"Oh, shut up, you old buzzard," Holt muttered and dismounted.

He stepped in Cami's direction, grabbed one of the wide brass horns of her longhorn belt buckle and hauled her in close. He lowered his head until their hat brims collided.

She stared up at him, her expression all sweet and innocent. The light flowery scent of her warred with the more familiar odor of sweat and horses. Lord, she was a pretty little thing. But pretty little things were about as welcome on his ranch as curds in the buttermilk. And for a damned good reason.

The last pretty little thing he allowed on his spread took him for every dime he had. And that clever maneuver almost cost him the ranch that had been in his family for 109 years. It had also forced him to open his ranch to dudes in order to pay the bills. His mouth tightened and he spoke quietly in her ear, determined to ignore the silky black curls that blew against his face and tickled his jaw.

"Listen up real close, *Tex.* You help those fine folks settin' on my porch get off it and on their way. And then you and I are going to exchange a word or two about that resumé you sent and that contract we signed. Got it?"

She nodded energetically, her brim clipping his and knocking both their hats askew. "Got it," she said. "I'll take care of it right away, boss." She swung around, the wickedly curved horn on her buckle catching him in the gut and snagging his shirt.

"Son of a—"

The sound of rending cotton and popping snaps brought her up short. "Oh, dear," she said with a gasp and turned back.

"Whoa, Nellie!" Holt dodged a swipe from the opposite horn, moving away before she could do any real damage.

"Put a rope on that maverick she's wearing," Gabby suggested, "before it turns you from a bull to a steer."

Holt examined his gaping torn shirt and the long, angry scratch scoring his stomach. Anger stirred. "Tex?" he murmured. "This is not a good start to our relationship."

She gulped, her gaze fixed on his injury. "Is that...*blood?*"

He took one look at her suddenly white face and slapped a hand to the scratch. "No, it's not," he lied without compunction. "It's ooze."

"But . . . it's red." She swayed. Gently. From side to side.

"Right. It's red ooze." As much to distract her as for his own peace of mind, he held out his free hand. "The buckle, Tex. Give it over," he ordered, staring at her implacably.

A hint of color returned to her cheeks, his diversion tactics apparently working. "But my pants . . ."

"Those britches of yours have enough starch in them to stand on their own. They'll stay up just fine, belt or no belt. Now give it to me before you put someone in the hospital."

With a great show of reluctance, she unhooked the belt and slid it through the loops. "I'm real fond of this buckle," she murmured wistfully. "I've dreamed of owning a buckle like this for a long, long time. Don't you like it?"

Now she'd done it. Gone and made him feel like a heel. A heel making a fuss over a little bitty nothing of a scratch. Shoot. "It's a fine buckle," he found himself saying.

He avoided looking at Gabby and Frank. He knew if he did his two companions would get to laughing and he'd be forced to discourage them—undoubtedly with his fists. Matters would slide downhill from there, and more ooze would be spilled. Plain and simple, keeping his attention focused on Tex seemed the wisest course of action for all concerned.

"Really?" she said. "You really think it's a fine buckle?"

"A buckle like that demands respect. A lot of respect." He glanced downward at his torn shirt again. "And a lot of distance."

She peered at him hopefully. "Then I can keep it on?"

He wasn't that stupid. "No."

She sighed, handing over the belt. "Okay. You're the boss."

"You got that straight." He held the thing gingerly by one horn and jerked his thumb toward the family of redheads. She took the hint.

She jangled onto the porch and faced the Radburns with an encouraging smile. "Okay, boys, everybody grab a suitcase or bag and haul it to the car." Rhonda clung to the arms of the rocker and moaned.

"Can't we stay here?" Rufus demanded. "I wanna be with you."

Cami ruffled his hair. "I wish you could, buster. But it seems you belong next door. Now get going. Rollie, you let that mouse out of your pocket before you get in the car. Rob? Think it'll be too much trouble to reassemble that roof rack?"

"Not at all. I'll get right on it, Cami." He hustled toward the car.

"Rhonda, you come with me, honey. Now, now. Whimpering won't solve anything. Give me the baby. Heavens, looks like there's been a flood south of the border. We'll have him changed in no time."

Holt watched in amazement as, without missing a step, she plucked the diaper bag from the pile of luggage, settled the wriggling baby on top of a canvas tote and commenced to buff, puff and dust. In no time, she'd restored a cooing infant to his mother's arms and convinced the contrary woman to return to her car. Once they were settled, Cami poked her head in the window.

"Here you go, boys. Take my yo-yo and do some practicing. I've got plenty more where that one came from. I expect next time I see you, you'll put me to shame with the stunts you can do. No, no, Rusty. Bopping your poor momma is not a good trick." She pulled back and waved. "Don't be strangers, now. We're just one big, happy family around here. So, you come and visit real soon. Hear?"

"Well, now," Gabby muttered. "If that don't beat all."

Frank nodded in agreement. "Wish I could stick around and see if she's as smooth a wrangler as she is a talker. But I better start for home. Once my housekeeper gets a load of those Radburns, she's gonna up and quit on me. No question about it."

Holt gave them a look of disgust. "Nobody who dresses like that has been within spittin' distance of a ranch, and you both know it." He folded his arms across his chest. "She's no wrangler. I'd bet my bottom dollar on it."

His gaze wandered in her direction. No, he realized grimly, she wasn't a wrangler, but she *was* trouble. He didn't doubt for a minute that that girl could sweet-talk a chicken out of the jaws of a starving coyote. He didn't intend to let her sweet-talk him. No sir. Not him.

And yet... Doggone it. With all that black hair hanging past her shoulder blades in tight, shiny curls, even the back of her appealed. Not to mention her nipped-in waist, a pert little rump and long, lean legs that could clamp around his saddlebags any day of the week. She was too pretty by half, he judged. Which meant the only way to protect himself was to get her off his ranch. Pronto. Before she had a chance to open her mouth and change his mind for him.

She turned and practically sashayed across the dusty yard to his side. He forced himself to be fair. With those ridiculous chaps and jeans, sashaying was probably the only way she could move. He spoke before she had the chance. No point in giving her an unfair advantage. "I'm calling your bluff, Tex. Time to put up or pay up."

She didn't seem the least concerned. "I'm ready when you are," she said.

He gave an abrupt nod. "I'll go find your resumé and we'll get this nonsense over with." He strode toward the ranch house and snagged his foreman by the arm. "Get Petunia," he ordered in a quiet aside.

Gabby started. "Petunia? You sure?"

Holt risked a quick look over his shoulder. She stood in the middle of the drive as soft and fresh as newly churned butter. He almost changed his mind. Almost. Then her dimples winked at him. "Just do it!" he barked, slamming his hat down on his head.

Hell's bells and little fishes! he thought as he stomped up the porch steps. That woman was yanking his chain something fierce.

And the worst part was, she didn't even know it.

CHAPTER TWO

CAMI WAITED IN THE MIDDLE of the deserted yard, watching Gabby strike out for the barn and Holt disappear into the ranch house. This, she decided, was the moment of truth. Here she stood, in the midst of a hostile environment, able to count on one person and one person alone. Herself. In a short while she'd be faced with a set of near impossible tasks—a challenge she could not and would not refuse. It was a challenge she'd face dead on, never once flinching no matter how rough it got, just like the gunslingers of the Old West.

She stretched out her arms and laughed aloud. Lordy, she loved being a cowboy!

Several minutes later Holt Winston returned to the porch, a roll of papers crumpled in his hand. She simply stood and stared, overcome with admiration. He'd shoved his Stetson to the back of his head, revealing dark brown hair shot with streaks of sun-ripened gold. Without the shadow cast by his brim, she could also see his face more clearly, and she liked what she saw.

His features had none of the smooth, boyish charm of so many of her male friends. The weathered crags and valleys of Holt's face revealed a man who'd lived hard and on his own terms, who'd known his fair share of sun, dust and wind. A starburst of tiny lines emphasized his unwavering gaze, and deep creases bracketed a firm mouth and square set chin. From the high jutting cheekbones and uncompromising blackness of his eyes, she suspected Mexican or Indian blood had found its way into his ancestry.

He'd changed his torn shirt, she noticed with some relief, the heavy denim free of distressing blood specks. His fleece-lined vest blew open in the breeze, revealing a pair of work gloves tucked into a wide black belt. His leather chaps rode low on his hips, clinging to his long, lean legs and emphasizing the fluid grace of his movements.

Here before her stood an honest-to-goodness cowboy. He was tall, spare and muscular. And absolutely perfect. How she envied the life he'd led...the life she'd always dreamed of leading.

"Don't just stand there," the honest-to-goodness cowboy groused. "Haul your citified tail over to the corral and let's see what you can do. Or like as not," he added beneath his breath, "can't do."

"Yessir, boss," she said, trotting after him. This was it. Her big chance. Boy howdy, it didn't get any better than this!

Gabby exited the barn, weighted down by a saddle and blanket and leading a large dun mare. He gave the horse a light swat on the rump and it trotted into the corral. With the ease of long practice, he swung the saddle onto the upper rail of the fence and climbed up next to it.

"All set," he called.

Holt nodded, slapping the resumé and references against his thigh. "Says here you're quite impressive with a rope," he addressed Cami. Snagging a length of thick braided manila off a post by the corral, he tossed it to her. "Try impressin' me."

The rope uncoiled, half the length slithering in the dirt. This wasn't a problem, she decided, gathering up the excess. She'd impress him. Sure she would. Besides, how hard could it be?

Holding the bulk of the rope in her left hand, she swung the looped end into the air and twirled it. To her utter delight, not to mention amazement, it worked. A large spinning circle appeared above her head. She looked over at Holt and grinned.

"Where'd you like it, pardner?" she drawled.

"Lasso the post next to Gabby. The post," he emphasized, "not my foreman."

"You got it." She snapped her right arm back and then forward, toward the post. The rope obediently flew off behind her. It never reappeared. Instead, the rope went taut and she heard an anguished howl. She whipped around and stared in horror.

"Congratulations," Holt said. "You roped my sheepdog. Any time we need Git hog-tied, I'll know who to call."

"Lord have mercy!" she exclaimed, running for the dog. Gently she eased the rope from around the animal. He gave her hand a pitiful little lick and flopped onto his back. "I'm sorry, Git," she said earnestly. "Truly, sorry."

Holt strolled over and peered down at the dog. "I do believe he surrenders. If you can convince the cows to do that, we've got it made." He eyed her sternly. "Now, would you care to tell me what you do with a rope that's so all-fired impressive?"

"Hang swings," she admitted.

"Come again?"

She cleared her throat. "I...I hung a couple swings for the neighborhood kids. Their parents were very grateful. When I asked for references, they were happy to oblige.''

"You're kidding."

"Am not. I have a real knack for knots, too. And one other thing." She dug deep into her pocket and pulled out her spare yo-yo. "I can rope something fierce with this."

"The hell you can."

She looked him straight in the eye and said, "The hell I can, too."

"That's not even a rope," he scoffed. "It's a string."

She shrugged. "Rope, string. It's all the same. Only difference is the thickness."

He shoved his hat back on his head, clearly put out. "I'd call that a rather significant difference. Wouldn't you?"

"No. Just watch."

She jumped to her feet and stood a comfortable distance from the post he'd wanted her to lasso. Planting one heel firmly in the dust, she gave the yo-yo a few warm-up spins. Ready, she jerked her wrist and sent the yo-yo flying toward the post. It whistled by Gabby, spun around the post and tied in a pretty knot.

Gabby nearly tipped off the railing. "Son of a . . ."

Holt folded his arms across his chest. "Is that what you plan on doing to my longhorns? I've got news for you."

Cami frowned. "It won't work?"

"Glad you agree."

"But don't you see? I'm a natural with ropes." She glanced at the yo-yo. "Okay, with strings. But I can graduate to ropes. I know I can. The only difference is—"

"Thickness. So you said. Fact is, I need a wrangler who's already good with ropes. Not with yo-yos," he said, stemming her attempts to argue. "With ropes."

"Strike one?" she asked.

He inclined his head. "Strike one. Let's see how you do with horses." He examined the papers in his hand. "Says here you're a natural with livestock and that you first sat a horse when you were three."

"True. Every word."

"Uh-huh. Well, don't just stand there. Go get your horse saddled."

Cami scuffed her boots in the dirt. Would this be the right time to point out that her resumé didn't mention anything about saddling horses? Perhaps not. Somehow she doubted Holt would appreciate the distinction. Besides, how hard could it be?

"Er, what's his—" She peeked at the animal's hindquarters. "*Her* name?"

"Petunia."

"Good. A Petunia." Anything named after a flower couldn't be too bad. "I can handle a Petunia. Sure I can." With a decisive nod, she struggled over the corral fence.

The horse stood ten yards away, swishing flies with her tail. Reacting to the jangle of spurs, the animal swung her head around and gave Cami the once-over. Apparently unimpressed, Petunia turned away with a noisy snort.

"Hey, there," Cami called. "Nice day, isn't it?"

The horse ignored her. Was it her imagination, or had the animal suddenly grown? Not that it mattered. Huge or not, she'd have to find a way to stick a saddle on its back and climb aboard. Catching the reins, she led Petunia over to where Gabby sat with the saddle. He tossed her a pad and blanket.

Okay. A pad and blanket. They undoubtedly went under the saddle so as not to give the horse saddle sores. Made sense. She could do this. But which came first? Pad or blanket? She struggled to recall and drew a total blank. No problem. When all else failed, use logic and reason . . . then guess.

She stepped in front of the horse, stroking the soft tan muzzle. Petunia ducked her head and Cami took the opportunity to whisper into the huge horsey ear. "Time for you and me to reach a little understanding. I need to look good and I'd appreciate your help with that. I've already struck out on my first cowboy skill. I'd be real sorry, if not downright annoyed, if I struck out on this one, too. So what do you say we girls stick together and make a small—though profitable—bargain? Say a lump of sugar in exchange for fifteen minutes' good behavior?"

Petunia snorted, grabbed a mouthful of silver shirt fringe and chowed down. Cami scuffled with the horse and came away with a bit less fringe than she'd started with. "That's a yes, right?" she asked. Petunia grabbed for more fringe and Cami darted toward the horse's midsection. "Well if that's a yes, I'd hate to think how you'd tell me no. But I'm willing to give you the benefit of the doubt. I guess."

"That horse ain't gonna saddle itself, no matter how long you stand there and jaw with it," Gabby complained.

"Gotcha," she said with an agreeable nod. "More saddle, less jaw."

Trusting to dumb luck, a quality that rarely let her down, she placed the pad first and the blanket second, across the horse's back. Great. She scratched her head. Not great. There seemed to be a whole heck of a lot more blanket than horse. This couldn't be right. The deep creases in the thick cotton caught her attention and inspiration struck. She folded the blanket and eyed the results. That looked much better. She returned for the saddle.

"Allow me," Gabby said. He straddled the rail, grabbed the saddle horn, and passed her the saddle.

"Too kind," she said. She grasped hold of it, staggered beneath the unexpected weight and measured her sixty-seven inches in the dirt.

Gabby chuckled. "Heavy sucker, ain't it?"

"I hadn't noticed," she claimed, struggling to get the saddle off her chest.

Holt leaned against the fence, his arms folded across the top rail. His shoulders quivered in a most suspicious manner. "Need help?"

"Oh, no. I'm doing just fine. Thanks."

She managed to get her legs beneath her and stand. Approaching the horse, she gave a tremendous heave. The saddle whacked onto Petunia's back, stirrups and straps flying. The horse snorted, kicking at the stirrup. Cami planted her hands on her hips, quite pleased with herself...until she noticed that the saddle horn pointed south, when it should have pointed north.

She sneaked a glance at Holt. Had he noticed? His shoulders quivered again, which probably meant he had noticed. Dang. She turned back to the horse.

A few twists and turns and grunts had the saddle where it belonged. Now for the hard part—getting it connected. Crouching, she peered beneath Petunia's belly at the two woven straps dangling from the far side of the saddle. Large brass rings decorated the ends.

Connected to the back strap ring was a beltlike contraption. Finally. Something familiar. Something that should be easy and straightforward. She darted under the horse and grabbed the back strap.

"Ahem."

Cami glanced at Holt. "Ahem?"

He nodded. "Ahem."

"Gotcha."

She let go of the one strap and grabbed the other, gently easing it beneath Petunia's belly. Now to figure where the darn thing connected. Striving not to appear as green as she happened to be, she poked and prodded. How did John Wayne do it in all his movies? He lifted something up and ...

Experimenting, she lifted a leather flap connected to the saddle and found a matching ring with several thongs attached to it. *Aha!* It only took a minute to wind the thongs from the one brass ring to the other. Last of all she tackled the back strap. This one proved easier still, fastening like a belt. Finished, she slapped the dust from her hands, proud as punch. She'd done it. She'd actually done it!

"You want me to mount up now?" she asked, facing the two men with a broad grin.

"Boss?" Gabby nodded toward Cami's feet. "Best get those spurs taken care of first."

Holt nodded. "Climb up on the fence," he ordered.

Somewhat awkward in her stiff new chaps, she did as he asked, while he strode over to Loco, waiting patiently in the shade. Unsnapping a leather holster buckled to the saddle, he pulled out a tool that looked like a cross between a pair of wire cutters and a hammer and carried it back to her perch.

"Hold on a sec." He grabbed her boot and twisted, snipping the long, sharp points off her spurs.

"Hey, there. Whatcha doing?" Cami cried in alarm.

"You aren't getting near Petunia with these on your boots. You'd cut her to ribbons." Once he'd snipped the spurs down, he bent in the sharp ragged edges. "Okay. Now you can mount up."

She climbed off the fence and frowned. Her spurs didn't jangle worth a darn now, but real cowboys learned early on to face adversity. And spurs that didn't jangle were a minor adversity—nowhere near as bad as losing her longhorn cow buckle.

She approached the horse with determination. She'd done a truly pathetic job at roping, worn the wrong kind of spurs and gotten the saddle pointed backward. She didn't want to embarrass herself further by getting herself pointed backward, too. She closed her eyes and pictured the dynamics involved in putting the proper foot into the correct stirrup in order to end up facing the horse's head rather than the horse's tail.

Satisfied with her game plan, she stuck her right foot into the stirrup and grabbed the horn, swinging her left leg up and over. The next instant, the saddle slid rapidly beneath her. She released a muffled shriek and clamped on with all her might.

Silence reigned.

Well, she'd done it. She was, indeed, facing the horse's head. Unfortunately she was facing it from the vantage point of the horse's belly.

Gabby exploded with laughter, toppling from the fence rail. Petunia ducked her head between her front legs and peered at Cami as if she'd taken leave of her senses—which in all likelihood, she had.

Familiar chap-encased legs appeared beside her. "Tex?"

She gulped. "Yessir?"

"You ever saddle a horse before?"

"No, sir. I sure haven't. And if you look real close at my resumé, I don't think you'll find any such claim."

"Trust me. I'll give it a real close look." He stooped. "You need some help?"

"Maybe a little," she admitted reluctantly.

He reached beneath Petunia and plucked her off the saddle by her shirt collar. "This does not bode well for your future as a wrangler. You realize that."

"Yessir. I do. Is this strike two?"

"You could say that."

He unhooked the saddle and tossed it onto the rail. "Pad first, then blanket. Shake them out, checking for burrs and lumps. They need to be smooth under the saddle," he explained as he went. "Place 'em high on the withers."

"High on the withers. Got it."

"Next comes the saddle. Hook the offside stirrup on the horn, so you don't clip her elbow, and put the saddle on her." He glanced down at Cami. "Horn in front."

"Horn in front. Got it."

Lifting the saddle off the rail, he dropped it onto the horse's back with an ease she could only envy. Next he ran a hand across Petunia's ribs. "Check her flanks," he ordered.

"Nice flanks."

He closed his eyes. "I'm glad you approve. You might notice, they aren't moving."

"No, they aren't," she agreed.

"Which suggests?"

"That she's holding real still."

He released a long-suffering sigh. "It also suggests she isn't breathing."

Cami stared harder at Petunia's flanks. "That doesn't sound good. Should we be worried?"

"I'm beginning to think so," he muttered. He jammed his hat down and explained, "She's holding her breath."

Cami nodded solemnly. "Me, too."

He ignored that. "You can't get a saddle on good and tight when a horse is holding its breath." He gave a significant pause. "Once she releases it, the saddle slips off."

"Well, I'll be!" Cami exclaimed. "That sneaky devil. She sure put one over on me. So what do we do?"

Holt grabbed the front cinch and clipped Petunia's side with his knee. The horse exhaled and he pulled the strap tight. In short order, he finished saddling. What had taken her twenty minutes to accomplish, he'd done in two.

He leaned against Petunia's side. "Like to give it another shot, or you want to concede defeat now?"

She drew herself up straight and proud. "You're forgetting I'm a Texan—tough as nails and danged stubborn to boot. I'll never concede defeat. Long live the Alamo!"

For the first time, a genuine smile eased his mouth. "You've got grit, I'll give you that."

"Thanks." She grabbed the reins and gave Petunia a conciliatory pat. "Don't forget our bargain," she warned the horse, and once again shoved her foot into the stirrup.

This time she gained the horse's back without further incident. Not bad, she decided. Anchoring her hat more firmly on her head, she steered Petunia away from the fence. This was it. Her final chance at the big time. She could do it, no sweat. Besides, how hard could it be?

With an enthusiastic "Hiyah!" she slammed her newly trimmed spurs into Petunia's sides. She realized her mistake a moment too late.

Petunia didn't take kindly to having spurs, trimmed or otherwise, slammed into her sides. With a shrill whinny, she launched straight into the air and landed with a bone-shattering thud. Still not having expressed her disapproval thoroughly enough, she took off like a shot. Cami bounced once in the saddle, once on Petunia's back and once on the ground, before skidding to a halt on her much-abused posterior. Her hat drifted down to settle at her side.

She struggled to her feet, spitting dirt. "I hope you realize this cancels our bargain!" she shouted after the horse. Reluctantly, she glanced toward the two men. Gabby had fallen off the rail again. Holt occupied himself staring at the ground. She picked up her battered pink cowboy hat and hobbled across the corral.

"Strike three?" she asked.

"Strike three," Holt confirmed. He lifted an eyebrow. "You sticking to that story about first sitting a horse when you were a toddler?"

She slapped dust from her hat. Feathers filled the air. "Yessir. I am."

"Uh-huh." He eyed her keenly. "I assume that was also your last experience sitting a horse."

"Yep." She offered a crooked grin. "But look on the bright side. At least this time I didn't break my arm when I got thrown."

"I'm so relieved."

She heaved a sigh. "Mr. Winston—"

"Make it Holt. You've earned the right to that, if nothing else."

"Thanks." She stared at him earnestly, wiping a trickle of sweat from her brow. "I know it doesn't seem likely, but I can do this job, given half a chance. I'm a fast learner. You only have to show or tell me things once for me to catch on. And I want this job. I want this job more than I've ever wanted anything."

A deep frown creased Holt's brow. Slowly he shook his head. "Sorry. There's a dozen dudes scheduled to arrive next week and I need a wrangler who can carry his weight."

"I can carry my weight," she insisted, forcing herself to meet his hard, unemotional gaze. "I can carry more than my weight if it means working on a ranch."

"'Fraid I'll have to pass."

He turned to leave and Cami knew she'd better talk fast, or her job would be over before it ever started. "Is there anyone else you can get on such short notice? At least give me a chance until you've found a replacement."

"You have my answer," he said without slowing his gait. Something in his voice warned her she was treading a fine line.

"If I haven't proved I can do the job by the end of those two weeks, I'll go," she said, refusing to give up. "I'll even refund my wages."

"No." He kept walking.

It was all-or-nothing time. A few more steps and he'd be gone... and so would her dreams. "Our contract provides for a two-week unconditional trial period," she called after his retreating back. "I'm asking you to stand by your word and give me every minute of those two weeks."

She saw him hesitate and she played her final card—the one that in ages past would have gotten her a bullet in the gut. "Or don't you stick by your word? I thought a cowboy's honor meant everything to him."

That stopped him. Slowly he turned around. With a low, menacing growl, he snatched off his hat and buried it in the dust. "That tears it."

"Head for the hills, girl!" Gabby yelped. He hopped off the rail and loped toward Holt.

Deciding the foreman had offered a decent piece of advice, Cami did some rapid backpedaling. Suddenly the corral seemed a whole heck of a lot smaller. At the rate Holt was advancing, she'd run out of retreating space real soon. Perhaps she shouldn't have played that last card with quite so much enthusiasm. "Um, Holt? Mr. Winston? Sir?"

He continued to stalk her. "You and me seem to have a small communication problem. I think it's time we cleared that up."

Gabby gained Holt's side and grabbed his arm. "Now take it easy, Holt."

"Yes. Let's take it easy," Cami agreed, with an urgent nod. "Very easy."

Holt shrugged off his foreman's hand. "Forget it."

"It was desperation talkin', not her," Gabby tried to convince his boss.

"Desperation," she said, tripping over her shiny new boots. "Absolutely. It was desperation."

Holt snagged a hunk of fringe and yanked her to a stop. "When I'm done with her, desperation won't do her talking ever again."

She stared in horror at his restraining hand and dug her heels in like the most ornery of mules, pushing against his pull. He let go and she stumbled, sprawling in the dust at his feet.

Petunia trotted over and shoved her muzzle into Cami's face. Cami shoved back. "Move aside, Petunia. He's gonna kill me, sure as I sit here. And I wouldn't care to have you caught in the cross fire."

Gabby danced at Holt's side. "She just wants to be a cowboy, is all. She didn't know what she was sayin'."

Cami frowned. Up until that moment, she'd been in complete accord with Gabby. Now she wasn't so certain. "Wait a minute," she said, scowling up at the two men. "If he's going to kill me, it might as well be for the right reason. I did mean what I said. I meant every word. True, desperation encouraged me to say it. But we signed an agreement, and I intend to make him stick to it."

"*What?* You...he...I..." Gabby sputtered to a halt and folded his arms across his chest. "I give up, boss. Go ahead. Shoot her."

Good, old Texan cussedness came to the fore. "Not until I've had my say." She pushed dark curls away from her face and spoke from the heart. "For my entire life, all I ever wanted was to be a cowboy like my poppa. I was born on a ranch. If my poppa hadn't died, I'd have been the sixth generation to grow up on Greenbush land. I know I'm a mite clumsy right now, but give me a chance. That's all I'm asking. You won't be sorry."

"I'm already sorry." Holt spoke roughly, but she sensed his anger had faded. He reached down and held out his hand. "Come on, Tex. As much as the thought appeals, I'm not going to shoot you. Leastwise, not today."

She took his hand and stood. "Can we come to some sort of compromise? You want a wrangler and I want a job. By the end of two weeks, I'm willing to bet we'll both be satisfied."

He mulled over her words. His gaze, hard and stern and unrelenting, met hers. "I need a wrangler who can groom horses."

"No problem."

"Ever do it?"

"Nope. But I'm strong and I'm determined and I've never been afraid of hard work. You show me how, and it'll get done."

"I also need someone who can saddle a horse and stay on it while riding."

"I guarantee, Petunia and I *will* come to terms."

"I believe you, Tex. But that still leaves me short a wrangler who can handle cows and knows how to rope."

She spoke with certainty. "Give me those two weeks and you'll have all that. Otherwise, I'm gone without a word of complaint."

He shook his head in disbelief. "You expect to learn everything in two weeks?"

"Just watch me." She peered at him anxiously. "Does this mean I can stay?"

Gabby grabbed Holt's arm and muttered, "No sense in turning away help, incompetent though it may be. Get some work out of her for all your time and trouble. Tomorrow you can phone around for a replacement."

Holt still didn't seem convinced. "Give me one good reason why I should let you stay," he said to Cami.

"I'll give you three. I like people and I like animals." She threw her arms around Petunia's neck. "And they like me."

Petunia snorted and swung her head, knocking Cami back on her keister. "See?" she exclaimed with a huge grin. "The exception that proves the rule."

Gabby rolled his eyes heavenward. "Lord Almighty, have mercy. Cuz we're gonna need a heapin' helpin'."

"Amen," Holt concurred.

CHAPTER THREE

THE BEDROOM LIGHT switched on, practically blinding Holt. He sat up cursing. "What the *hell* is going on?" he demanded.

"You awake?" Gabby whispered.

"I am now." Holt threw back his covers. It had to be serious for his foreman to wake him from a sound sleep. "What's wrong?"

"I'll show you, if'n you give me a minute," Gabby muttered. "I'm gonna turn the light off, okay? See if you can get over to the window without breakin' something."

"Worry about yourself, old-timer. I can make it just fine." The room went dark once more. Holt kicked his boots to one side and gained the window without barking his shin more than twice. Quite an achievement, considering his eyes were blurry slits and his brain hadn't clicked in yet.

"Now, real easy like, twitch that curtain apart," Gabby instructed, "and tell me what you see."

Holt looked and swore again. "Damnation, I don't believe it." He turned and glared at Gabby. "What time is it?"

"Four-thirty."

"*Four*-thirty? What the devil is she doing up at this hour?"

"Don't holler at me! You were the one who told her she better not be late on her first day of work," Gabby complained, yanking furiously at his mustache. "You also said, if'n she was, you'd fire her and t'hell with the contract. Those were your exact words. 'I'll fire you and t'hell with the contract.'"

"I remember, you old coot. You don't have to repeat it a hundred times." He glanced at her again and winced. Moonlight spilled over Tex, encasing her in a cold silver glow. Did she have to look so... lonely? So... vulnerable? So... *female?* He pulled back from the window. "Late for work does not mean four-thirty and she damn well ought to know that. It's ridiculous. She's got Petunia saddled and everything."

"Petunia don't 'pear none too happy about it, neither. Not that I blame the poor horse." It was clear from Gabby's tone whom he did blame.

"I can't help it if the woman has a burr under her saddle about being a cowboy."

"Oh, yes you can." Gabby folded his arms across his chest. "She ain't gonna be happy and outta here till she shakes that burr loose. And you're the man to help her do it."

The muscles tightened in Holt's jaw. "Fine. When I get up in another hour and a half, it'll be my pleasure to check her saddle blanket for burrs. In the meantime, I'm going back to bed."

"And leave her shivering out there? Look at her. Even her hat's got goose bumps."

"Those aren't goose bumps," Holt said in disgust. "She's plucked some poor chicken bald and filled her hat up with more of those danged feathers."

Unable to resist, he peered through the window again and frowned. He hated it when Gabby was right. And this time he was very right. Tex shook so hard she could probably register as a minor earthquake. Didn't she have more sense than to stand there in that cold spring wind? He was tempted to open the window and blister her ears with a few home truths. That would warm her up. And then some.

"Look on the positive side," Gabby said, peeping around Holt's shoulder. "At least she'll leave a trail if she ever gets lost."

Holt returned to his bed and sat down. "So long as that trail heads east, I don't give a hoot. Now get out of here and let me sleep."

"Now, now. Here's your boots."

"I don't wear boots to bed." His voice held a warning.

"You ain't goin' back to bed. You're goin' down to that little girl and teach her how to be a cowboy."

Holt glowered. "In case you hadn't noticed, she isn't a little girl. If your eyesight wasn't so bad, you'd be able to see that."

Gabby grinned. "I see jes' fine. You'd be amazed at how well I can see."

"You're getting on my nerves, old man. You best fetch clothes for yourself, because I won't be going alone. You're coming with me." He shook out his boot and shoved his foot into it.

"At this hour? What are you, loco?"

"Not yet. But it won't take much more to get me that way. Two weeks with her and they'll have to put a rope around me and drag me off to the loony bin."

"Well, until that fine day comes, you've got a job to do. And since you agreed to it of your own free will, you're stuck doing it all by your lonesome. You take care of Tex, and I'll take care of things around here."

"I agreed to it," Holt grumbled. "But I'm not so sure about the free-will part. Ever since that female showed up, I've been doing things I swore I'd never do and saying things I swore I'd never say. She's trouble, I tell you."

"Dang tootin'!" A slight flush streaked Gabby's weathered features. "You take one look at that long black hair and the silly dimples twitching in her cheeks and pow!" His fist connected with Holt's gut. "Gets you right there, don't it? Then she stares at you with those big blue eyes and you start to grinnin' and countin' those itty-bitty freckles perched on her nose and—"

Holt shot to his feet and glared at his foreman. "Never you mind those freckles."

Gabby held up his hands. "Take it easy. I didn't get far with them. Only up to fourteen. Why don't I go fix you a nice hot thermos of coffee."

"Fine." Holt snagged his hat off the bedpost.

Gabby made his way over to the door and cleared his throat. "Feed some to Tex, okay?" he said, before beating a hasty retreat.

Smothering a curse, Holt crushed his hat down on his head and stomped from the room. Somebody would pay for his irritation. And he had a good idea who.

CAMI SHIFTED CLOSER to Petunia, trying to absorb some of the horse's warmth. Lordy, it was cold. And dark. And lonely. She thought longingly of her bed. Another hour's sleep wouldn't go amiss, either.

Aw, quit your bellyachin'! This is what she'd waited for, what she'd wanted to do all her life. A bit of cold weather wasn't going to keep her from being a cowboy.

It might freeze her stiffer than a june bug in the Arctic, but it wouldn't stop her.

After a moment's hesitation, she unsnapped the rope from her saddle. A little practice while she waited wouldn't hurt anything. And it might warm her up. Now if she could only see what she aimed the rope at. She peered through the moonlit darkness.

"Wait here," she ordered Petunia, and moved off a few paces. No sense in roping her horse. Besides, she doubted this particular one would stand for it.

With a quick toss, she spun the rope over her head. That part, she had down pat. Now if she could get the throwing part figured out, she'd have it made. She gave the rope a few more practice twirls. Satisfied, she snapped her wrist back. Once again the rope sailed off behind her. Once again it snagged on something, refusing to reappear. And once again, Holt's sheepdog howled in anguish.

She turned and winced. "Tell me I didn't do that," she groaned, running to the animal's aid.

She dropped to her knees and gently loosened the rope. The sheepdog whimpered, shoving his cold, wet nose into her hand. "I'm real sorry, Git," she murmured, stroking his thick coat. "I hope you realize I didn't do it on purpose. I just can't get the hang of this roping business."

The dog gave her hand an encouraging lick, and with a quick apology for the delay she eased the rope off him. "Tell you what. Why don't you go stand over there by Petunia, and I'll try and rope something else."

The dog skulked toward the safety of the barn and Cami sighed. She couldn't keep roping that poor dog. She had to get this cowboying stuff right sometime soon, or she wouldn't meet Holt's criteria. And she had to succeed. She *had* to.

With renewed determination, she stood and walked to the middle of the yard. She tossed the rope into the air, spinning it in a smooth circle above her head. So far, so good. Now, a quick jerk of the wrist, and... To her exasperation, the rope flew off behind her and went taut. Something thudded to the ground and she heard the tinkling of shattered glass.

"You crazy female! What the *hell* do you think you're doing!"

Cami swiveled in her tracks. Lordy, lordy, lordy. She'd done it this time. She'd gone and lassoed her boss. And he seemed upset. Mighty upset. Fact was, he appeared hotter than kerosene put to a match. Her gaze moved to the thermos rolling at his feet. Another casualty, if she didn't miss her guess.

"The thermos?" she asked. "It's broken?"

"Bingo, Tex," he practically snarled.

The porch light snapped on and Gabby stuck his nose out of the door. He took one look at the damage, yelped, "Head for the hills, girl!" and darted inside.

With a smothered exclamation, Holt grabbed a piece of the rope wrapped around him and gathered up the excess, reeling her in. He stopped once they stood toe-to-toe and brim-to-brim. "You broke my coffee!" His breath smoked the air between them.

"I didn't mean to. Honest." She swallowed. Who'd have thought his black eyes could get any blacker? Not her! "Holt. Mr. Winston. Sir."

"I don't take kindly to people who break my coffee. I need that coffee. That coffee's the only thing that keeps me civil at four-thirty in the morning. Fact is, it's the only thing that's going to keep me from strangling you. And you broke it."

Her head bobbed up and down. "Yessir, I did. I don't deny it for a minute." She stared at him earnestly. "Holt?"

"What?"

"I'm sorry," she said with heartfelt sincerity. "Real sorry."

"You...I..." He gritted his teeth and she watched, fascinated by the play of muscles across his jaw. "Apology...accepted," he finally bit out.

Heavens, he was a fine-looking man. Even angry, there was an essence about him that drew her, spoke to her on a subconscious level. Did he feel it? Did he sense anything at all? She stared, captivated by the jet black eyes and the lock of gilded brown hair that tumbled across his forehead. Every line of his face revealed the strength and determination and drive that personified the man.

"What's this?" His eyes narrowed and he cupped her chin, tilting her face up to his. His brows drew together. "You're bruised." His thumb caressed her cheekbone.

Was that concern in his voice? "It's nothing." She shrugged off the injury, unable to shrug off her reaction to his touch as easily. It sparked a warmth deep in her belly. A warmth that took her by surprise. "If it makes you feel any better, I've learned it's best not to land face first when you come off a horse." She gave him a tentative smile, relieved to see a glimmer of humor appear in the sooty depths of his eyes.

His head dipped lower, and he turned her face to better examine her cheek. "You have bruises in less...visible places?" he asked.

Her smile widened. "Maybe one or two."

"You'll have more before the week's over," he warned. His hand slid slowly from her face, leaving behind a trail of liquid fire. "I've got cream that'll help. Be sure you rub it in well."

"Thanks. I—"

The door banged open and instantly Holt stepped away from her. Gabby scampered down the porch steps. "I got you more coffee," he said, holding aloft a new thermos. "No real damage done." He helped untangle Holt from the rope and shoved it into Cami's hands. "Best get this put away," he muttered in her ear.

"Thanks, Gabby," she said. "You're a sweetheart."

He reared back, glaring from beneath thick white brows. "Don't go gettin' mushy on me. If there's one thing I hate, it's mush."

Holt glanced from one to the other. "You two through sweet-talkin' each other? We've work to do."

With a noisy "Humph," Gabby shoved the new thermos at her, picked up the broken one and stomped into the house. Cami bit down on her lip to keep from laughing.

Holt nodded toward the coffee. "Drink some of that while I get Loco saddled. It'll take the edge off the cold."

She hesitated, reluctant to create further contention between them. "I'd be happy to, if it were tea," she admitted finally. "But I'm not overly fond of coffee."

He lifted an eyebrow. "You best get this straight right off, Tex. Real cowboys have two and only two beverages they drink—coffee and whiskey. And every once in a while, when they're pushed, they'll take a gulp of water to ease a dusty throat. But they never, *ever* drink tea."

"Got it. Coffee and whiskey. Ace out the tea." She peeked up at him, a teasing grin playing across her mouth. "Got any whiskey?"

"It's in with the coffee," he drawled, and started for the barn.

Cami eyed his retreating back. Furtively, she turned around and uncapped the thermos. In with the coffee? Was he serious? She took a cautious sniff. All she could smell was coffee. Pouring a bit into the top, she took a quick sip and choked. Dear heaven! This had to be the strongest stuff she'd ever tasted. And the worst. If it wasn't laced with whiskey, it ought to be, if only to dilute the coffee.

"Don't let it go to your head," Holt murmured from directly behind her.

With a cry of alarm she whirled around, coffee flying in all directions. Petunia, in particular, took exception to the bath and clipped Cami on the shoulder. The thermos tumbled to the ground, a quart of spilled coffee rapidly turning the dirt to mud.

Before she had a chance to move, let alone speak, the ranch-house door slammed open and Gabby tumbled down the steps. "Couldn't help but notice what happened. And it's the strangest thing," he called as he trotted across the yard. "Just happened to have this extra thermos all ready to go."

"Thanks," she said with a relieved sigh.

"Quite a coincidence," Holt said grimly.

"Yeah, well..." Gabby scowled at Cami. "I have a feeling we're in for a lot more such coincidences."

He deposited the thermos in Holt's hands, snatched up the one lying on the ground and retreated toward the house. "Thought I'd fill in for Agnes till she returns. I'll make us a stack of my flapjacks. You get along with the chores and I'll have the griddle sizzlin' hot when you're ready to eat."

The door banged shut behind the foreman and Cami glanced uncertainly at Holt. "Sorry about that," she murmured. "I guess you surprised me."

"Likewise." A hint of irony crept into his voice. "It might be smart if you and I kept our distance."

She eyed him speculatively. Maybe it hadn't been her imagination after all. Maybe he had felt something when he'd touched her. If it was even close to what she'd felt... "It would be safer, that's for sure," she muttered.

Amusement gleamed in his eyes. "Agreed." Turning away, he crossed to Petunia and checked her cinches. With a satisfied nod, he said, "Okay. Mount up. We'll go get the *redondo*." At her confused look, he explained, "The workhorses. We bring them in from the pasture and take a curry comb to them. Once that's done, we'll try Gabby's cooking."

"And then?"

His smile made her nervous. "And then we start work."

"TODAY, I'M GOING TO take it easy on you," Holt announced.

"That's what you said yesterday," Cami griped good-naturedly. "And now that I think about it, that's what you said the day before, too. Your taking it easy is liable to kill me deader than a cockroach beneath a fly-swatter."

"Ready to give up and go home?"

"No way." She shifted in the saddle. "I gotta admit though, I have blisters in spots I didn't know I had skin *to* blister."

He shot her a quelling look. "Real cowboys don't blister."

"Maybe you should explain that minor detail to my tailbone." She grimaced. "Not that I'm complaining. If cowboys don't blister, I'll stop blistering. Any minute now." She peeked over her shoulder at the part of her planted in the saddle. "I hope."

Holt cleared his throat. "About today's work..."

"Don't keep me in suspense. How are you taking it easy on me today?"

"By riding fence."

"Great." She glanced at him from beneath her hat brim. "Doesn't that hurt?"

A grin creased his lean face. "Only when you sit down. Come on. We've fence lines to check." He nudged Loco into a trot.

The sun broke above the mountains before her, tinting the snow-topped peaks with varying shades of pink and purple. She caught up with him before he cleared the next rise. "I never noticed before, but these mountains have faces," she said in surprise. She pointed to a huge craggy one off in the distance. "See that pointy one?"

"They're all pointy."

"The one way in the back. With the mustache. It looks just like Gabby. The snow hangs off that ridge the same way his droopy ol' mustache hangs off his face. And see that top part? Those are his bushy eyebrows. I'd know them anywhere."

"You have a mighty vivid imagination, for a cowboy." Holt dismounted and dropped his reins to the ground. He snagged a fallen section of barbed wire and stretched it to the nearest post, hammering it in place.

"You'll find those hills take on a whole new appearance with each season."

"Wish I could be here to see it." She leaned across the pommel and watched him. His efforts pulled his cotton shirt tight, the muscles across his back and shoulders rippling with each blow of his fence tool. "I can't get over how beautiful this part of the country is."

He spared her a quick glance. "You haven't been out here before?"

She shook her head. He'd touched on a sore subject, one she'd always been reluctant to discuss. "Aside from Texas, I haven't been anywhere but Virginia. And to be honest," she admitted in a low voice, "I barely remember Texas. I was three when we left."

He tipped back his hat and rested his forearms across the top of the post. She read a sympathetic warmth and a certain gentle humor reflected in his dark eyes. "That would be after you fell off your horse and broke your arm?"

Cami laughed. "Yep. Right after that." Her smile faded. "Actually, Momma decided to return to Virginia when Poppa died. So, I spent my entire growing-up years there." She shrugged carelessly, hoping to conceal her pain. "Sad, but true."

She could tell she hadn't fooled him. He wiped a trickle of sweat from his brow, giving her a moment to collect herself. "If you grew up back East, explain the accent," he demanded, steering the topic onto a more neutral course.

"I'm a Texan," she said kindly. "The accent's a birthright."

"Like your cowboying skills?"

She ignored his dry tone. "Exactly. I haven't had the opportunity to use those skills, is all. Which is why they're a mite rusty. But don't you worry. I'll catch up faster than buckshot chasing a varmint's tail."

His lips twitched. "Tell me something ..."

"If I can."

"Why wait so long to act on your cowboy birthright?"

She frowned. "Momma ... Well, let's just say that Momma wasn't suited to ranch life. It would have hurt her something fierce if I'd up and left. I couldn't put my own self-interest first. But this seemed the perfect solution." She ticked off on her fingers. "It's temporary. It'll give me the opportunity to see if I'm truly suited to the life. And it fulfills my dream."

"And if it ends in two weeks?"

She gave him a level look. "I'm like my yo-yo. I may take to spinning and getting tied up in knots, but I always come back."

"Which means?"

"Which means that if this doesn't work, I'll try again. And again. And again. Eventually, I'll get it right." She tugged her hat lower on her brow. Feathers burst from the hatband, caught in the breeze and spun in little circles around her head. "But you know what?"

His dark eyes glittered with laughter. "What?"

She firmed her chin. "I'm not leaving in two weeks. And, mister, you can bank on that."

The humor faded from his eyes and he straightened away from the fence post. "Banks in these parts have a history of folding. You'll have to excuse me if I prefer to wait and see."

He climbed onto Loco and hesitated. With a muttered exclamation, he reached into his saddlebags and rummaged for a tube of lotion. "Haul your tail over

here, Tex. You forgot to lather up that nose. You're
starting to look like Rudolph."

Cami urged Petunia closer and held out her hand. To
her amazement, he snatched off her hat and hung it on
his saddle horn. Then he squeezed a generous dab of
zinc oxide onto his finger and with great care smeared
the ointment across her nose. "This sun has given your
freckles freckles." His voice dipped lower, acquiring a
rough edge. "Lots of bitty pinprick freckles."

She froze, his tone unsettling her, reviving that ten-
sion-filled awareness. He was so different from the men
she knew. Tough. Lean. As strong and intimidating as
the mountains around them. And as impervious. She
was out of her depth... and knew it. She eased away.
"Thanks."

He dropped her hat back onto her head and a few
more feathers bit the dust. He nodded in satisfaction.
"Won't be long now."

She stared at him in confusion. "Won't be long till
what?"

"Until that hat starts looking like a hat again, instead of something out of a chicken's worst night-
mare."

"You don't like my hat?" she asked, insulted.

"I like it just fine. Except for the color and the
feathers. Hats should be black or brown, and feathers
belong on birds."

There didn't seem to be an adequate response to that.
Holt turned Loco east along the fence line and after a
moment, she followed. They dipped into a deep ravine,
muddy from spring runoff. At the bottom, he drew up
short.

"You hear something?"

She listened carefully. "Sure do. Sounds like some-body's crying." She pointed toward thicker brush. "That way, I think."

Single file, they picked a path through the scrub. In a small clearing they found a cow and her calf. The calf was bawling its head off. The cow, bogged down in mud, simply stood looking miserable.

"What do we do?" Cami asked in alarm.

"We pull out the cow," he said, matter-of-factly.

She couldn't conceal her relief. Of course. They'd pull out the cow. She knew he'd have the perfect solu-tion. A sudden thought occurred and she frowned. "How do we pull her out?"

"With a rope."

"Good. A rope. We have ropes. This will work." Holt continued to sit and study the cow's predicament and Cami gazed at him in concern. "Well, what are we waiting for? That poor baby looks half-starved. Let's get to it."

He sighed. "It's a calf, not a baby. And it probably is half-starved. But the first thing to learn about cattle, Tex, is you don't go in half-cocked. In case you hadn't noticed, cows are big and heavy and dumber than a rock. You need to decide the safest way to handle the situation. Then you do it."

She nodded decisively. "No problem. Plan first. Ex-ecute plan second. Tell me what you want and it's yours."

"It can get tricky, so do exactly as I tell you," he in-structed her in a stern voice. "Understand?"

"Yessir, boss."

"I'm going to wade in and pull the cow's legs loose. Once that's done, we need to put a rope around her horns and haul her out."

He shed his gloves and dismounted. Gingerly he entered the mud hole, sinking in up to his knees. Keeping a weather eye on the distressed animal, he worked his way around her, shoving his hands along her legs and carefully lifting them free of the mud. The cow rolled her eyes and bellowed, struggling against the pull of the ooze.

Cami watched anxiously. She couldn't just sit and do nothing. She had to help. City slickers sat around without a clue. Like Holt said, cowboys—real cowboys—formulated a plan and took action. That decided, she freed her rope and twirled it carefully overhead.

Take it easy. Don't screw up. Snagging the bushes won't help the cow. And more than anything, she wanted to help. This time she took care not to snap her wrist back, but used the natural impetus of the rope to throw it forward. The loop flew through the air and dropped cleanly. Unfortunately it dropped over the wrong animal. With the immediacy of long practice, Petunia danced backward and the rope pulled tight. Holt measured his full six-foot-three-inch length in the muck.

"Whoa, stop," Cami shouted, bouncing in the saddle and digging her heels into the horse's sides.

Petunia, seeming to have a mind of her own, ignored the order and continued in reverse. With a loud slurping, sucking sound, Holt popped out of the mud hole and slid across dirt and rock. The horse shifted into neutral.

Slowly Holt stood. All she could see were two black eyes glaring from a mountain of mud. The mountain of mud whipped off the rope and threw it down. She swallowed. Hard. He took a step toward her and she burst into panicked speech.

"Gee. I'm real sorry about this, Holt. Mr. Winston. Sir."

"Get . . . off . . . that . . . horse."

"You see, Petunia got it into her head to back up and I couldn't stop her."

"Get . . . off . . . that . . . horse . . . now!"

"Yessir. Right away, sir. You think we should get that cow out first? I mean, as long as I'm up here and you're down there all muddy and every—"

"*Get off the fool horse, woman!*"

She tumbled off Petunia. "Oh, Holt. It's awful. I was just trying to help. Honest, I was. And you said we had to rope the cow. *We.* That means both of us. Like . . . you *and* me. So, I thought, why not me? You were busy pulling the cow's legs from the mud. You couldn't do that and rope at the same time. Which left me to do it. So I did. Only I missed. And you . . . I . . . Petunia wouldn't stop. I said, whoa. I said, stop." She glared at Holt. "Doesn't your horse understand English?"

He started for her and she belatedly shut her mouth, deciding that a full retreat was in order. Before she could back out of reach, he grabbed a fistful of shirt with mud-coated hands. The next instant she found herself plastered up against him, stuck tighter than a bug on a strip of flypaper.

His hard, muscular thighs rode her softer curves, his wide shoulders eclipsing her view. His chest heaved and his breath came fast and furious. He seemed to have trouble speaking, but she suspected that wouldn't last long.

She was right.

"You and me are going to come to an understanding, Tex," he informed her through gritted teeth.

"You got it. Anything you say." She peeked up at him hopefully. "Um...do you think we might come to this understanding with a bit more distance between us? Remember? For safety's sake?" She wriggled tentatively. Slippery curves slid over taut, sinewy muscles. It was the wrong thing to do.

She froze. He groaned.

"You haven't been safe from the minute you hit Winston land." His head dipped lower. "And neither have I."

And with that, he kissed her.

CHAPTER FOUR

EVEN THOUGH HE WAS covered with mud from top to toe and all points in between, Holt's kiss was the most marvelous Cami had ever experienced. In fact, if her boots hadn't been in the way, his kiss would have knocked her socks clean off. As it was, he knocked her hat into the dirt. Not that she cared.

She tilted back her head, wrapped her arms around his neck and enjoyed. His mouth clung to hers, rough in a passionate sort of way, though not in the least hurtful or insensitive. He'd done this before, she could tell. And he'd learned to do it real fine, too. For an instant she considered telling him so, but she couldn't seem to gather her wits sufficiently to speak.

He eased his grip on the front of her shirt, his hands sliding upward to cup her face instead. They were strong hands, hands as quick to calm any misgivings as they were to curb any opposition. Not that she offered much opposition. Heavens, no! Why would she fight a touch as smooth and warm as good whiskey? Especially when his brand of whiskey licked through her veins with dizzying speed.

She sighed against his mouth, totally passion drunk.

To her eternal frustration, he chose that moment to pull away, his touch no longer easy and caressing, but hard and inflexible. She resisted. She held on and resisted with every ounce of her strength and determination. Heck, even their shirts resisted—cemented together as they were by drying mud. Unfortunately, he was stronger...and more determined. With a popping of shirt snaps, he set her from him. For a long moment they simply stood and stared at each other, his breath as fast and gusty as hers.

"I shouldn't have kissed you," he admitted, putting more space between them and folding his arms across his gaping shirtfront. Mud oozed down, painting the solid muscles of his abdomen a rich dark brown.

Cami swallowed, struggling to turn a blind eye to such an irresistible sight. It proved an impossible task. The temptation to close the distance separating them almost bested her. For the first time ever, she found herself at a loss for words.

Lordy, what should she say? That he could kiss her anytime he cared to? That she didn't mind if he kissed her silly? That she *wanted* him to do it again...and soon? She shifted beneath his cool, remote scrutiny, dropping her gaze to her pointy-toed boots.

Spying her hat, she bent and picked it up, twisting the brim between nerveless fingers. Tarnation! Wasn't this a fine mess. She glanced at his filthy clothes and that tantalizing glimpse of naked chest. A fine mess in more ways than one.

"I gather you don't make a habit of kissing your wranglers?" she finally managed to say.

"No, I don't. And if you'd been a man, I'd have knocked you on your backside for pulling a stunt like that." His black eyes continued to burn with a strange intensity. "But since you aren't a man..."

"You kissed me." They couldn't avoid the truth. The sooner they faced facts, the sooner...what? What happened now? Did they ignore the kiss and put it behind them? She wasn't certain she could. Did they pretend the kiss never happened? It would take a heap of pretending, that was for darn sure.

"I shouldn't have touched you," he stated baldly. "It won't happen again. I don't kiss my employees, nor do I kiss city slickers. And you qualify on both counts."

She flinched at his harsh tone. "I may be your employee, but I'm no—" She broke off at the look on his face. She'd never seen him so cold and distant. She'd stumbled onto something here, and instinct told her she'd better find out what. "What's wrong with kissing city slickers?" she asked instead, dreading his response.

For a minute, she didn't think he'd answer. Then he said, "The cost is too high. Last time I kissed one, I ended up married to her. That mistake almost lost me my ranch."

She stared in shock. "You're married?"

"Divorced."

Divorced. Of course. It made perfect sense. It explained his flashes of anger and bitterness, she thought with compassion. It also explained his attitude toward her, both for being a woman and for being fresh from the city. "And because of that one experience, you hold a grudge against all city slickers?"

"Good guess, Tex." He picked up her rope and tossed it to her. "Our arrangement isn't working. You realize that, don't you?"

Panic-stricken, she shook her head. "No, I don't realize it. I'm a little green, I admit. But I can do the work. I know I can."

He crushed down his hat, his jaw assuming a rock-solid set that suggested he'd made up his mind, and come hell or high water he'd stick to it. "No, you can't.

You've proved that here today. You're more hindrance than help.''

"Dropping you in the mud was an accident," she protested.

A grim smile eased the lines around his mouth. "If I thought otherwise, we wouldn't still be talking. You'd be packed and on your way by now, sorer but smarter." He snapped his shirt closed and snagged his rope off Loco's saddle horn. "The fact remains, I don't have time for your brand of accidents. I have guests arriving in a couple days."

She nodded enthusiastically. "Great. I can't wait."

"Not great. There's work to be done that isn't getting done. You're holding me back. I need someone experienced enough to get a solid day's work under his belt—"

"*His* belt?"

"His or hers, makes no nevermind to me," he replied coolly. "So long as they do the job and help train the newcomers, that's all that matters. You can't do either. I spend more time bailing you out of trouble than I would the damned dudes. You're dangerous, Tex. Putting someone like you on a ranch is just asking for it."

Desperation tinged her voice. "I'll get better. I know I will."

He didn't give an inch. "Not on my ranch, you won't. And not on my time."

"But—"

He stopped her with a single cutting look. "I have enough hands to cover the general ranch work—baling hay, hazing cattle, that sort of thing. And I have a couple of women who will take care of the guests' children. What I want and what I need is a wrangler who can help Gabby and me with the dudes. That's an experienced, honest-to-goodness, knows-what-he's-doing wrangler I'm talking about. I don't have the patience, nor the inclination, to play cowboy with you."

"Great. Because I'm not playing!" she shot at him. "You're tromping on sacred ground here. Cowboying is serious business to me, not just a game. I'm here and I'm here to stay."

Two swift strides brought him to her side. He towered over her. "Wrong. You're here because I'm a man of my word. I signed a contract with you and I'll honor it. You'll have your two weeks. But once those two weeks are up, you're gone. And nothing and no one is going to change my mind."

"Unless I meet your conditions, you mean," she was quick to say.

"Not likely, Tex." Grim certainty marked his expression. He pointed at the mud hole. "See that cow? My job is to yank it free and return it to the herd. A cowboy—a *real* cowboy—would have helped me drag her outta there by now. Instead, I'm still picking mud from between my teeth."

"I said I was sorry about that. It's my fault you got a little dirty. I admit it."

"A *little* dirty?"

"Okay," she conceded. "A *lot* dirty. But as far as wasting your time—" She took a deep breath and plunged onward. "You didn't seem in any all-fired hurry to get down to business once you slid out of that hole."

"You're walking a thin line here," he warned.

"I don't doubt it for a minute. But that doesn't change the facts. As I recollect, you had other concerns on your mind after you got up close and personal with that mess of muck." She tilted her chin to a reckless angle, daring him to disagree. "And not one of them had a blessed thing to do with helping that poor cow."

"What's your point, Tex?" he snarled.

She continued doggedly. "That my being inexperienced isn't why that cow's still sitting rump deep in mud. You were the one sidetracked, not me. You were also the one doing the grabbing."

He whipped his hat off his head and slammed it into the ground. "That tears it . . ."

Cami gulped. Maybe she'd gone a tad too far with that last remark. She took a hasty step back. Not that it helped. He swallowed the distance between them in one swift stride. She looked up at him. Boy howdy, was he tall. And hopping mad, too.

"Excuse me there, Holt," a laughter-filled voice interrupted.

Holt froze in his tracks, slowly swiveling to face the newcomer. Cami peeked around Holt's back, surprised to see his neighbor, Frank Smith. The rancher had a shoulder propped against his horse and his arms folded across his chest.

"Been there long?" Holt demanded.

A knowing grin eased the lines of Frank's tanned face. "Long enough. Thought maybe before you get to killing your wrangler, you might like some help pulling that cow out of the mud," he offered. "Then you can strangle the girl or shoot her...or whatever else you had in mind."

The muscles in Holt's jaw tightened and Cami caught a brief glimpse of the fury still sparking in his dark eyes. A long minute ticked by before he gave an abrupt nod. "Fine. Let's get to it."

Frank straightened and tossed his reins to Cami. "Take the horses off a piece. It wouldn't do to be anywhere nearby when that cow gets on her feet." He joined Holt, addressing him in a low voice. But a sudden gust of wind gave Cami full benefit of his words. "You know, it's just my opinion, but if you don't want folks to know what you two have been up to, you best learn not to leave fingerprints."

Cami flinched and stared down at the front of her shirt. An ample helping of mud coated her clothing, along with two telltale handprints where Holt had grabbed hold of her shirt. That hadn't been the only place he'd touched, she suddenly remembered. He'd cupped her face, too. Surreptitiously, she rubbed her cheeks and looked at her hands. Streaks of mud stained her fingers. Dismayed, she glanced at Holt to check his reaction to Frank's comments.

Not that Holt's expression told her anything. It was as if he'd shut off all thought and emotion. Without a word, he picked up his hat, slapped it on his head and climbed on Loco. One easy spin and toss of his rope and he'd lassoed the cow's horns. A moment later, he'd pulled her free of the mud. She lay on her side, bawling miserably.

Frank joined Holt and studied the cow. "She doesn't look like she's going to get up on her own."

"Nope," Holt concurred. "Tex, come get Loco. Ground hitch him over yonder. Hear?"

With a nod, she led Loco to where the other horses stood.

Holt caught hold of the cow's tail. "Let's tail 'er up. Get the horns. Ready?"

"Set," Frank said.

At Holt's nod, they both lifted and flipped the cow onto her feet. She immediately tried to charge Frank. Holt, his heels dug into the ground, held her back by the tail.

Once Frank was safely to his horse, Holt let go. The cow appeared uncertain what to do next. The bawling of the calf seemed to be the deciding factor. She trotted over to her offspring. Holt kept behind the animal and edged across to Frank and Cami.

"Go back to the ranch and get cleaned up," Holt instructed.

"What about you?"

"I have work to do."

"But..."

He tensed, his hands balling into fists. "Don't argue with me!" He was clearly at the end of his patience. He took a deep breath, struggling to rein in his temper. "Go to the ranch and get cleaned up," he repeated in a low, stern voice.

Deciding to follow the prudent course for once in her life, she nodded obediently. "Yessir. And then?"

"We'll get the cow and calf back with the rest of the herd down by the river. You can join us there."

"Yessir," she repeated and climbed aboard her horse.

With a shrill "Giddyup!" she wheeled Petunia around and dug in her heels. The horse took off like a shot. This time, Cami clung to the saddle with all her might. Judging by the look in Holt's eye, falling off meant death. And most likely a slow one, at that.

HOLT WATCHED CAMI CHARGE through the bushes and up over the ridge, shiny black curls bouncing against her back. He remembered sliding his hands through that hair and the feel of her curls beneath his hands. The softness had taken him by surprise, the little ringlets twisting around his fingers, clinging and twining so he'd been afraid he'd hurt her when he'd gathered sufficient wits to pull free.

"You've got trouble," Frank said.

"Big trouble," Holt concurred.

"So what are you going to do about it?"

"Keeping my damned hands off her might be a good start."

"A difficult proposition."

"A painful proposition." They both fell silent for a few minutes. In a resigned voice Holt asked, "I don't suppose you've heard of any decent wranglers looking for work."

"I put the word out. The few I heard were free I wouldn't have within a thousand miles of my spread. What about those other resumés you received? Isn't there anyone else you could hire?"

Holt shook his head. "Only one was available and she was eighty-two. I'd have hired her on the spot, but she'd just been released from the hospital following a bout of pneumonia and the doctor wouldn't okay it."

"Which leaves Tex."

"Which leaves Tex and all that damned black hair," Holt agreed.

"And those big blue eyes."

"Not to mention the dimples."

"Or the freckles."

Steel crept into Holt's voice. "Mention those cute little freckles in that tone and I'm like as not to knock you on your arse."

"You've got trouble."

Holt yanked his hat low on his forehead. "Big trouble."

CAMI WALKED TO THE SIDE of the ranch house and into the laundry room. Holt had shown it to her the day she'd arrived and told her he'd recently put in sufficient machines to service the hands as well as the guests. "Feel free to use it anytime," he'd said. "You'll get plenty dirty working around here." He hadn't been kidding.

She bypassed a long folding table covered with a pile of heavy-duty commercial towels, several pairs of faded jeans and a neat stack of flannel shirts. Crossing directly to the washing machine, she opened the lid and dumped in her muddy clothes and a cupful of detergent. Her mouth curved downward.

Here she stood, squeaky clean from head to toe and poor Holt was out on the range with mud-filled boots, a dusty hat and a six-inch coating of muck. By now the muck would have dried beneath the warm spring sun into something akin to plaster. If he hadn't been cemented in place atop his horse, he'd at least be itchy and miserable . . . and ticked.

And it was all her fault.

With a sigh, she started the washer and turned to leave. Feeling guilty wouldn't help. Nothing she could do would help, except, perhaps, to stay away from ropes, mud holes and Holt. And considering that cowboying on the A-OK frequently involved all three, her future looked decidedly dicey.

It was time to get moving. Time to return to work. Time to give Holt more of her special brand of help. She hesitated, her gaze falling once again on the stack of clean clothes lining the folding table. Inspiration struck. Maybe, just maybe, there was something she could do to make amends.

Snatching up jeans, shirt and a towel and washcloth, she headed for her horse. Shoving her collection into the saddlebags, she mounted. "Come on, Petunia. Let's find Holt. He sure is going to be pleased when he sees what I've brought him."

They'd be working down by the river, he'd said. To her surprise, she found him in the first pasture she crossed. She pulled up short and watched, her brow wrinkled in confusion. What in the world was going on? Frank and Holt, whistling and hi-yahing for all they were worth, busily pursued a bunch of longhorn cows.

She took another look. Those weren't just cows they were attempting to corral. The herd contained a huge infuriated bull, as well. Cami winced as a wickedly curved horn slashed a path inches from Holt's thigh. This was no place for an amateur to be, she realized, deciding to sit tight. The last thing Holt needed right now was a distraction. And without doubt, she seemed to have an uncanny knack for distracting, not to mention riling the man.

An instant later, a huge longhorn thundered by, pointed straight at Holt's back. On the other hand... Reacting instinctively, she clipped her heels against Petunia's rump and gave chase. She reached for her rope and hesitated, an image of this morning's disaster flashing before her eyes. The longhorn continued on its path of certain disaster and Cami realized she had to act fast. If she didn't stop that beast, Holt would be on the hurting end of those horns.

Without further consideration, she shoved her hand into her pocket and yanked out a yo-yo. Petunia increased her stride, until they were just behind the cow. Cami hollered a warning to Holt. He whirled around, but she knew it was too late for him to escape those huge horns. She let fly with the yo-yo.

The bright red yo-yo spun to within a hair of the longhorn's nose and jerked back, looping around and around one horn. Cami slipped the string off her finger and pulled Petunia up short. The cow bellowed a protest and skidded to an abrupt halt, inches shy of Holt. The yo-yo dipped and bobbed, dangling from one horn like a giant earring. Completely distracted, the longhorn stood, front legs spread wide, and shook its head, attempting to rid itself of this new annoyance.

A split second later, Holt cut between her and the irate cow, swiftly guiding her clear of harm's way.

"She was going to gore you. It was the only thing I could think of to stop her," she explained breathlessly. "I didn't dare use my rope. Not after this morning. Like as not, I'd have lassoed you or Loco instead of the longhorn. And I didn't want to hurt the poor thing, just get her attention off you."

"Fast thinking, Tex," he soothed. "I don't doubt for a minute that you saved my hide. Stay right here. Don't move from this spot. Understand?"

"Sure thing, but—"

"We need to finish corralling that bull and get him to his own pasture. Do not," he paused, holding her gaze with a severe expression, "do *not* help."

Her head bobbed up and down. "Yessir. No sir. I'll wait here and not be a bit of help."

Pulling his neckerchief over the lower half of his face, he pivoted Loco around and disappeared into a thick cloud of cattle dust. She watched anxiously for Holt and Frank to reappear. Eventually they did, guiding a struggling bull into another pasture. Securing the gate, they rode toward her.

"Is everything all right now?" she asked, noting their grave expressions. "What happened?"

Holt took his time answering. He removed his hat and wiped his sweaty brow with the back of his hand. His eyes, angry and dust rimmed, finally turned in her direction. "You see that bull?" he said, gesturing toward the animal ramming the stuffing out of a large cottonwood tree in the far pasture.

"I see him," Cami nodded.

"He's a Hereford bull. He's part of the herd raised for beef. See those longhorns?" He pointed to the cattle a short distance away.

"Yes, I see them," she repeated, more warily this time.

"Those are very expensive show cows. I culled them special and stuck them here because they're ready to be bred. Someone," he continued, "and I can't say for sure who that someone is—but *someone* left the gate open between the Hereford bull and longhorn cows. Do you realize how much money it'll cost me if that bull sires an offspring with one of my longhorn?"

She gulped. "No."

"Believe me when I tell you it's a lot." He leaned across his saddle horn, fixing her with a gimlet stare. "If I ever found out who left that gate open, I'd be tempted to shoot the varmint. Because only a varmint would be dumb enough to do such a thing. Especially in these parts."

"Why especially in these parts?" she whispered.

"Because in these parts the first lesson kids learn when they crawl out of their cradles is to keep the damn gates shut. First lesson. Shut the gate."

She bit down on her lip. "Got it. Shut the gate. Shoot the varmint."

"Perhaps Tex should call it a day," Frank suggested.

Holt inclined his head. "Good idea."

She glanced from one to the other. "But... but I'm all clean and ready to get dirty again." She clambered off Petunia and flipped open her saddlebags. "Besides, look what I brought you." She pulled out the towel and washcloth. "I figured you'd be dirty and itchy from all that mud and could use the river to clean up. And see..." She yanked out his jeans and shirt. "I even brought a change of clothing and everything." She frowned at the empty saddlebag. "Well, maybe not *everything*. I sort of forgot the soap. But that dirt should come off with a spit and a polish."

"Tex..." Holt began.

She clutched his clothes to her chest and peered up at him hopefully. "Yes?"

He cleared his throat. "Thanks. That was mighty thoughtful of you. There's one or two more chores I need to see to. It's a one-man job, so consider the next few hours off as a... a sort of bonus."

Her gaze dropped to her toes. "A bonus," she murmured. "Right. Much obliged."

He reached down and tugged the shirt, jeans and towel from her arms. "I appreciate your bringing these to me. I'll be along in a bit."

Without another word, she mounted and turned the horse toward the ranch house.

"Tex?"

She reined Petunia in. "Yes?"

"Don't forget to close the gates behind you," he said gently.

Cheeks burning, she gave a quick nod. A feather drifted from the hat brim and landed on the tip of her nose. "I won't forget," she assured, blowing irritably at the feather. "Shut the gate and shoot the varmint."

Keeping her spine ramrod stiff, she trotted Petunia across the pasture. She didn't even attempt to steal a backward glance as she passed through the gate and carefully and deliberately closed and latched it behind her.

CAMI LAY IN BED in the cabin assigned to the female hands. So far, she had the place to herself and she didn't like it. It felt cold and lonely. She stared out at the starry night, unable to sleep. A huge moon filled the narrow window, nearly blinding her.

Some cowboy she'd turned out to be. Tears filled her eyes and she gritted her teeth, fighting with every ounce of determination to hold them at bay. Texans were tough, she reminded herself. Texans didn't give up, no matter how difficult it got. Her poppa had taught her that. She squeezed her eyes shut. If Poppa could only see her now. His pride and joy. His little cowboy. The phrase joggled a distant memory and slowly it surfaced.

She'd been tiny. Very tiny. And sitting astride her very own pony. She'd made a successful circuit around the corral and her father had held out his arms to her. "Come here, Camellia-bush," he'd said with a laugh. "What a good little cowboy you're gonna make. Daddy's little cowboy."

Daddy's little cowboy. Oh, yeah. He'd be real proud if he could see her now. A tear spilled free, curving across her temple and soaking into her hair. With a muffled sob, she rolled over and buried her head in her pillow. Real proud.

CHAPTER FIVE

CAMI STOOD NEAR the corral, practicing her roping. Twelve days of her fourteen-day trial period had passed and it was fast becoming apparent that she held the only optimistic outlook about her future at the A-OK. Not that she couldn't change those other less-than-positive viewpoints. Unfortunately, it would take time—something in distressingly short supply.

On the plus side, she'd taken to grooming, riding and mending fences just fine. She grimaced. Okay. If she were honest, she'd admit she could groom and saddle Petunia, keep mostly atop the horse when riding, and string barbed wire without getting stuck more than six or seven times. On the minus side, she couldn't for the life of her get the hang of roping. And that was a big minus. Because until she did, her job remained in jeopardy.

Not that it wasn't anyway.

Ever since the mud hole and gate incident, her days on the range had been few and far between. Even now, Holt and Gabby were off together taking care of various "one-man" jobs. They never had adequately explained why, if these were one-man jobs, it took two men to do them. And if it took two men, why she couldn't be one of the two, freeing up the other for the real one-man jobs.

Oh, she'd asked, all right. And they'd hemmed and they'd hawed and they'd muttered beneath their breath a whole lot and shuffled in the dirt enough to raise a miniature dust storm. Gabby had turned a bit pink about the ears. And a frown as black as a thundercloud had darkened Holt's face. He'd slammed his hat low on his brow, and said "Just because, dammit," as if that ended the discussion. Then he'd wheeled Loco around and taken off before she'd had a chance to put him straight.

Worse was Agnes, Holt's housekeeper. She'd returned three days ago from vacation and had made it clear that the ranch house was off-limits to "hands," especially hands who weren't worth their salt and were citified to boot. Set on a course guaranteed to aggravate, she kept shaking her head and grumbling about "history repeating itself" and "there goes the ranch." That in particular had stung.

But most frustrating of all was knowing that the first batch of guests was expected any time and she, unlike all the other wranglers, didn't know what to do when they arrived. Not that she hadn't been told...

"Keep out of the way," Agnes had sniffed. "I'll take care of the guests."

"Show 'em your yo-yo tricks," Gabby suggested. "Jes' don't bean nobody."

"Give me your rope," Holt ordered. "I can't have you dragging any of the guests through the mud."

"Aw, Holt," Cami had replied in a mortified undertone. "Don't ask me to give up my rope. How am I going to meet your conditions of employment if I can't practice with it?"

He started to speak, then changed his mind. "Fine. Keep the rope. But stay away from anything that breathes. Got it?"

"Got it."

Now she stood, feet planted firmly in the dust, determined to practice until she collapsed. Not that it did much good. The closest she'd come to roping something was when she'd dropped the blasted loop on top of herself. But she wouldn't give up. No, sir. Not her.

For the fiftieth time that day, she swung the lariat into the air and tossed it toward the corral. For the fiftieth time it spun out in front of her. To her utter amazement, this time it dropped neatly over the fence post. A quick tug and it pulled tight. Son of a gun! She stood for a moment, staring in disbelief. A slow, wide grin split her face and she whooped for joy. She'd done it! She'd lassoed what she'd meant to lasso.

So what if it couldn't move, let alone moo. Once she got the hang of roping fence posts, roping cattle would be a snap. Holt would be impressed. Gabby would be amazed. Agnes would be speechless—finally. And Holt would sweep her up into those strong, powerful arms of his and twirl her around.

He'd say wonderful things like: "You're hired for the season. And by the way, this calls for another of those mind-splintering kisses." He'd duck down and capture her mouth with his. Romantic music would swell from speakers hidden in Gabby's mustache and she and Holt would ride off into the sunset searching for cows to rope. Life would be perfect again.

As if her success were a predetermined signal, a car pulled into the drive and a man and woman climbed out and looked around. From the back seat tumbled a little girl no more than five. Agnes appeared on the porch and greeted the couple. The little girl, after giving the housekeeper the once-over with a shrewd and discerning eye, abandoned her parents and skipped over to Cami's side.

"Hi. My name's Tina. This is my first time on a ranch. We had to drive hours and hours to get here. I almost threw up three times. Mommy has a headache and Daddy said a nasty word." She took a quick breath and clasped her hands behind her back. "What's your name?"

"Cami."

Tina stared, her shiny brown eyes filled with awe. "Are you a *real* cowboy?"

Cami stood a little straighter, tucked her thumbs into her belt and rocked back on her heels. "Sure am."

"Can you rope and ride and shoot and everything?"

"Well . . ." Cami strode over to the fence post to retrieve her rope. "To be honest, I can't shoot," she admitted.

The little girl appeared momentarily disappointed, but she made a quick recovery. "Will you show me how to rope?"

Another car pulled into the drive. Two boys and a girl crossed to Cami's side, their parents joining Agnes and the first couple on the porch.

"You gonna rope something?" one of the boys demanded.

She hesitated, recalling Holt's rather pointed instructions to keep her rope away from anything that breathed. She glanced from the eager faces gathered around her, to Agnes nattering on the porch with the adults. One little toss couldn't hurt, could it?

"Well, ah, I guess so," Cami said. She gathered up her rope and stood next to the children. Swinging the loop into the air, she peered down at them and grinned. "Now don't get in the way. And whatever you do, don't go off behind me."

She aimed for the corral fence and tossed. For the second time, the rope dropped dead center over the post. It was all she could do not to jump up and down for joy. She'd done it! She'd actually done it! Twice! Over the hill beyond the corral she saw Holt and Gabby riding toward the ranch. Had they seen her? she wondered guiltily. She shook the rope loose and reeled it in, wrapping it around her arm as she did so. With any luck, they hadn't.

"Do it again! Do it again!" the children clamored.

"I don't know," Cami said, reluctant to go borrowing trouble. Obeying Holt warred with her desire to show him how much she'd improved. If he could see her actually lasso something, maybe he'd keep her on as his wrangler.

"Please!" they begged. "Once more?"

"One more time and that's it for now," she said, and twirled the lariat.

She peeked Holt's way. She could tell by the sudden jerk of his head and the way he straightened in the saddle that she'd caught his eye—and that he'd taken note of the children at her side. To her dismay, Loco's pace picked up significantly. Did he really consider her such a hazard? Well, she'd show him. She'd prove herself. Boy howdy, would she prove herself. She twirled the rope for all she was worth.

"Oh, look!" Tina exclaimed, as Cami started into her throw. "A sheepdog."

It proved just enough of a distraction. Reacting without thought, Cami snapped her head to watch as Git slinked by. The rope, acquiring a mind of its own, snaked through the air. It landed clean again. Only this time it landed clean over Git. The sheepdog, literally at the end of his rope, howled in anguish and took off at a dead run.

Cami's horror made her reactions a shade too slow. Before she had time to drop the rope, it twisted around her arm and yanked tight. *This can't be happening,* she had a split second to think, before Git's momentum jerked her off her feet and onto her belly. She yelped at the unexpected and painful meeting of rock against rib.

"Whoa, Git!" she shrieked. "Stop!" To her everlasting relief, he obeyed. He skidded to a halt and turned to face her. Cami gulped.

This was one annoyed animal.

She stripped the rope off her wrist before he could take it into his head to run again. "Now, Git," she began, slowly backing away and holding up her hands. "It was an accident. I swear." He was having none of it. With a furious bark, he stalked her. "I'm sorry," she tried to placate him. "Truly sorry."

He didn't look convinced. In fact, he appeared bigtime ticked. A rapid retreat seemed in order. With a quick "Excuse me, folks!," she spun on her heel and ran. She darted around the hay wagon and into the barn, Git at her heels. She raced past the stanchions, manure gutters and troughs to the ladder at the far end. Dogs couldn't climb ladders, right? Lordy, she hoped not. She climbed. Fast. Git stood, paws planted on the bottom rung and barked.

Gaining the top of the ladder, she flopped onto the bales of hay, gasping for air. Whew! That was a close one. Not that she blamed the poor dog. Goodness, no. She'd be the first to admit she'd proved a bit of a trial for him. And until today, he'd been very patient. But all critters had their breaking point. She understood completely. She also understood that Git had reached his.

She nibbled on a fingertip. Now to explain why she'd taken to hiding in the hayloft to Holt. Somehow she suspected that wouldn't be too easy. A low warning growl brought her head up and she shot to her feet. So much for dogs not climbing ladders. This one had managed just fine. She retreated.

"Now, Git. I'm sure we can work a deal. Let's be reasonable. How about a doggy biscuit?" He kept coming and she kept retreating. "Okay. How about two? Three? You're really serious about this, aren't you?"

He stopped and sat, scratching furiously. Cami relaxed. "Good boy. Good Git." She offered her hand. "Wanna be friends again?"

He seemed to consider. It didn't take long. Giving in, his tail twitched into a wag and his tongue lolled out of his mouth. With an enthusiastic bark, he bounded toward her. Relieved, she took a final, unthinking step backward to brace herself against the arrival of sixty pounds of playful dog. It was a bad move.

Empty air greeted her booted foot. She teetered on the edge of the open loft door, scrambling for purchase, her arms pinwheeling madly. Git bounced up and gave her a forgiving lick. It was all the extra help gravity needed. With a shriek, she tumbled in a general down-and-out direction. *This is it. I'm dead,* she thought wildly. Her last sight was of Git standing at the loft door, staring at her, his head cocked to one side and a wide grin spread across his doggy mouth.

With a loud poof, she hit something reasonably cushy, something that broke her fall and closed around her, burying her in a bristly embrace. Cami opened her eyes, realizing she couldn't see a blessed thing. A strange thundering sounded in her ears, growing louder and louder. Then silence—an eerie, waiting sort of silence.

I've died. I've died and am floating through limbo. Scratchy limbo, but limbo. I see a light ahead of me. I'm drifting toward the light. It's growing brighter. And brighter. I can see now. I see...

Holt stared down at her from Loco's back, a clump of hay in his hands. She coughed on bits of dirt and debris.

"Is this heaven?" she asked in dazed wonder.

"Nope. It's hell in a hay wagon, Tex. Leastwise, it will be when I get done scorching your tail feathers." He reached into the wagon, shoving hay off her.

"Maybe I should explain..."

"Maybe you shouldn't. Stop wriggling, Tex. Let me make sure there's nothing broken." He checked her limbs with an impersonal touch and nodded in satisfaction. "You'll live," he informed her, though the blatant fury deepening his voice made her suspect he'd hoped otherwise. "You can thank your lucky stars you landed in the hay wagon and not three feet to the left or right. Of course, by the time I'm finished with you, you may wish you had missed the wagon altogether."

The next thing she knew, he'd snatched her up onto Loco and cradled her in his arms. She sighed and collapsed against him as they trotted across the yard. She should be worried. She should be nervous. Instead she grinned like an idiot. "If this is hell, heaven must be incredible," she mumbled, snuggling deeper into his arms.

"Pull it together, Tex. End of the line."

He plucked her from the saddle and planted her on the ground. She swayed, struggling to anchor herself on legs that had unexpectedly turned to mush. A dozen frightened faces spun before her dust-blurred eyes.

"Hey, there. Nice meetin' you folks," she said in greeting. Her knees buckled. "You'll forgive me if I don't stand, won't you?"

Holt leapt from his horse and wrapped a supporting arm about her waist before she hit the ground. "Hang on another minute," he murmured in her ear. In a crisp carrying voice, he announced, "Welcome to the A-OK Corral. We hope you enjoyed our little stunt show. It's our way of welcoming you to the wild and woolly west."

There was a moment of silence before relieved laughter broke out. "A show! Of course, a show," the guests commented to one another. They applauded enthusiastically. A moment later, the more astute of the ranch hands followed suit.

"Give them a wave and a smile," Holt instructed in a forceful undertone.

She obeyed, then tried to go one better. She bowed. It was a big mistake. The world tilted upside down, black dots obscuring her vision. Swearing beneath his breath, Holt scooped her into his arms and slung her over his shoulder.

"Happy to have you here," he said, pumping hands as he edged his way through the press of people. "Tex is going to get cleaned up and will be back real soon. In the meantime, Agnes can tell you where to take your bags." With that, he pushed through the last of the guests, climbed the porch steps and disappeared into the ranch house.

"Dang!" she moaned. "My ribs hurt."

"The state of your ribs should be the least of your worries," he growled. "You're lucky you weren't killed."

"Aw, Holt."

He continued down the hall and shoved open a door at the far end. It was a bedroom, she noted. A very stark masculine and upside-down bedroom. He set her carefully on her feet. With swift, economical movements, he slipped off her hat and nailed one of the bed knobs with it. His own followed ringing the opposite bedpost, the two hats spinning in identical lazy circles.

"Of all the stupid, idiotic stunts! What the *hell* were you thinking?" he snapped, dropping to his knees in front of her and unbuckling her chaps.

She shoved at his hands. He shoved right back. "That would be hard to say," she admitted.

"I'll bet. Because you weren't thinking, were you, Tex?"

"Could we skip that question and move on to the next?"

His shoulder clipped her hip and she toppled onto the bed. "Not tonight, dear," she groaned. "I have a headache."

"That's not the only thing you're going to have. Honey."

He tugged off her boots and stripped her chaps from her legs, tossing them to one side. She made a passing attempt to straighten her clothes, but he stopped her.

"Give it up. Your modesty's already shot to hell. All this shirt's good for is the ragbag. And that's being generous. Besides, I've seen women's undergarments once or twice before."

"Not mine you haven't."

"I'll try and contain myself," came his dry response. He peeled back the dirt-streaked ripped cotton and released a long, gusty sigh. The fury faded from his face. "Good grief. You sure do take this cowboying business to heart."

"That bad?"

A small frown appeared between his eyebrows and the muscles in his jaw tightened. "I've seen worse," was all he said. He traced her rib cage, probing with gentle fingers.

It was more than she could bear. She shivered, wriggling beneath his callused touch. "Cut that out," she complained. "You're taking advantage."

His hands stilled and a quiet laugh broke from him. "You call this taking advantage? No, Tex. When I take advantage, count on it, you'll be able to tell the difference. Now hold still. I want to check for damage."

"Damage?" If she didn't miss her guess, damage meant cuts and scrapes. And cuts and scrapes often leaked. And that type of leaking usually came in the form of vile and gruesome red splotches. She closed her eyes, unwilling to look for fear of seeing something that might make her woozy. "What's the verdict?"

"A few scratches. And you've got a nasty bruise on your side."

She risked a quick peek. "I seem to recollect a small skirmish with a rock."

"A losing skirmish, by the look of it. Nothing some soap and water and a few days' rest won't cure."

"I don't have a few days to rest."

"You do now."

She stared at him in distress. "Holt—"

His expression might have been carved from granite. "Don't start in on me, Tex. You'll come out on the losing end."

She eased onto one elbow, wrapping the remaining bits of shirt around her chest. "It was an accident."

He inclined his head, a shaft of afternoon sun highlighting the strands of gold in his brown hair. "It always is with you."

"I wanted to show you how well I could rope," she tried to explain.

"Oh, you did that all right."

"You don't understand." Enthusiasm entered her voice. "I nailed it, Holt. You should have seen me. I roped the fence two whole times!"

His eyebrows rose. "You roped the fence. Twice."

She beamed. "Sure did. And I would have done it a third time if I hadn't been distracted." She bit down on her lower lip, suddenly remembering. "Poor Git. I hope he's not still mad."

Holt folded his arms across his chest. "Last I saw, he was chewing your rope into scrap. That dog's going to be rope shy for the rest of his natural days. I should just shoot the poor mutt and put him out of his misery."

Wincing, she struggled to her feet. "You wouldn't," she said, appalled at the mere suggestion.

"He'd probably thank me for it." He thrust a hand through his hair and glared at her. "Turn off the waterworks, Tex. You know I wouldn't shoot Git. Come to think of it, the one I should shoot is you."

She bowed her head, overcome with remorse. "Are you very angry?"

"Very," he said in an uncompromising voice. "You disobeyed a direct order. And I take a dim view of employees who can't even follow the simplest of instructions.''

"Is there any way I can make amends?'' She glanced at him, fascinated by the sudden gleam in his dark eyes.

"I could come up with an idea or two, if pushed.'' He took a step closer and dropped his hands on her shoulders. "What the hell am I going to do with you?'' he muttered.

Nervously she shifted backward and lost her balance yet again. The bed provided a much more comfortable landing than the hay wagon. Holt followed her down, his hands braced on either side of her so he wouldn't bring further harm to her bruised and battered ribs.

For a long moment, he stared at her. She saw in his face the battle he fought, one between anger and desire. She knew the instant desire won.

"You've got eyes the color of a summer sky,'' he murmured. "And your smile's like a tiny ray of sunshine.'' He swept the curls from her face, tracing her high cheekbones with a surprisingly delicate touch. "It's been a long time since I last saw sunshine.''

"Maybe you were looking in the wrong place,'' she suggested.

"Maybe I just wasn't looking.'' He slid his hands into her hair, his thumbs stroking either side of her jaw. Never taking his gaze from her, he eased down, bracing himself on his elbows so his weight was a soft brush of leather and cotton against her breasts.

Without a word, he bent his head and kissed her, a rough, searching kiss. She groaned, wrapping her arms around his neck. "Are you taking advantage of me now?'' she whispered.

A laugh rumbled in his chest. "I'm sure doing my best.''

"I appreciate that." She raised her mouth to his. "I don't suppose you'd care to take further advantage?"

"My pleasure."

It was a long time before she surfaced. And then it was only because her enthusiasm overrode common sense. A sharp jab of pain reminded her of her less-than-perfect physical condition and she winced.

Holt's reaction was instantaneous. He rolled off her. Did he feel regret? she wondered. She studied his shuttered expression, searching for a clue to his thoughts. She came up empty.

He glanced down at her, a lock of gilt-edged hair tumbling across his brow. "I hurt you. I'm sorry."

She shrugged awkwardly. "Don't be."

In a swift, easy move he gained his feet. "Time to get you cleaned up." She started to stand, but he shook his head in warning. "Sit still."

"I can do it," she insisted.

He raised a single eyebrow, pinning her with a stern, cool gaze. She sensed the return of his anger. But who was he angry at? Her, for her free-fall into the hay wagon? Or himself, for having followed his more basic instincts? Probably a bit of both. Not that it mattered. She'd receive the brunt of his fury, regardless.

"You don't listen too good, do you, Tex?" he snapped. "Let me make myself crystal clear. Stir at your peril."

Considering how every muscle in her body protested the slightest movement, she decided he'd offered some sound advice. She lay back down. She ached from her belly flop into the mud puddle. But more painful still, she ached with a need so great it hurt to breathe. She suspected the latter would be the more lasting of the two.

Holt disappeared through a doorway and a moment later she heard the sound of running water. Unexpected tears filled her eyes and she shut them, fighting an acute sense of despair. Perhaps her injuries were worse than she'd suspected. How else to explain this sudden weakness? A moment later, Holt lifted her in his arms.

"Okay. Let's go," Holt said, crossing to the bathroom. There he thrust her, fully clothed, into the shower.

"Oh, good golly," she said with a sigh, enjoying the flood of warm water that poured over her. Her thick coating of dust turned rapidly to mud, pooling at her feet. Bits of hay dripped from her hair.

"Tex," Holt called. "It's time we discussed this problem you have with ropes."

"You'd like to discuss it here? Now?"

"Here and now. Help yourself to shampoo and soap."

"Thanks, I will." She reached for the plastic bottle and squirted a dollop of shampoo into her hand. It lathered up easily, smelling pleasantly of cedar and spice. "About my roping skills..."

"Or lack thereof."

"You, ah, you'd prefer me to keep away from ropes from now on?"

"'Fraid so. It's only for two more days. After that our contract will be satisfied and you can practice all you'd like. On somebody else's property, that is."

Cami bowed her head, suds dripping from her hair onto her shirt. What else had she expected? Had she really believed his kiss meant something? Had she really believed he'd want her to stay? "Is there any way I can change your mind?" *Please, say yes. Please.*

His response came in a hard unequivocal voice. "Not that I can think of. I'm sorry, Tex."

Her heart sank clear to her toes. "Me, too," she whispered.

"Tex?"

"Yes?"

"I'm going to get you a change of clothes. Don't go anywhere, hear?"

"Yessir. No, sir."

With that, the door closed behind him and Cami was left to her misery. She stood beneath the warm spray, a bar of soap clutched to her chest. So what did she do now? Concede defeat? Give up and go home?

Frowning thoughtfully, she rubbed the soap into what remained of her shirt. She still had two days. She'd have to find a way to prove her worth to Holt. She'd force him to see he was making a huge mistake. But how? She set her mouth in a firm line. Texans were tough. Texans were determined. She'd find a way.

CAMI'S LAST DAY ON THE job dawned clear and bright. Desperation marked her expression. This was it. Today she'd prove herself to Holt. Come hell or high water, today he'd hire her on a permanent basis. All she had to do was rope something without hurting anyone. Then he'd realize she could do the job and she'd become his official wrangler for the summer. That decided, she snagged a length of manila off the corral fence, determined to practice. Within minutes every child on the ranch had gathered round.

"Whatcha doing, Cami?"

"You gonna rope Git again?"

"Could you tie us up instead?"

Cami grinned at her following. "Practicing roping skills is serious cowboy work. You all stand clear and let me get on with my job."

Obediently they stood to one side, calling the occasional word of encouragement. Just as she tossed the rope for the third time, Tina screamed. Cami glanced from the rope to the child. No way had she done anything this time. Absolutely, positively, no way.

"Cami! Snake!" Tina finally managed to shriek, pointing at the ground. Coiled inches from the little girl's feet was a huge rattler.

"Get back!" Cami ordered the other children. "Go for help. Hurry!" She turned to Tina. "Now, sweetheart, don't move. And try not to be afraid. I'm right here with you. But you have to promise me you won't budge so much as an inch."

Tears filled Tina's big brown eyes. "I promise," she whispered. "Please, make it go away."

Urgently, Cami cast around for something—anything—with which to save Tina. Sweat beaded her brow. She had to think fast. She had to act now. Any minute the child would panic and run and the snake would strike. Her gaze fell on a shovel leaning against the barn and she could have wept with relief.

She addressed Tina once more. "I'm going to get something to hit the snake with, but don't worry. I'll be back in a sec. *Don't move.*"

With that she darted for the barn, snatched up the shovel and raced to within clubbing distance of the snake. "Close your eyes and hold real still," she instructed. Aiming carefully, she brought the shovel down on top of the snake in a single powerful blow. Moving with lightning speed, she swept Tina clear and, for good measure, smacked the snake a half-dozen times more.

Cautiously, she raised the shovel and peered at the snake.

Across the yard, Holt and Gabby came running, the other children at their heels.

"The kids said there was a snake. Where is it?" Holt demanded.

With a shaky finger, Cami pointed, then threw the shovel from her, her gesture one of loathing. She turned and buried her face in Holt's shirt. She couldn't bear to look at what remained of the critter. Holt's shirt—heck, Holt's arms—seemed a much safer place to be. "Did I kill it?" she asked his top button.

"Dead and then some," he confirmed.

She risked a quick peek over her shoulder and shuddered. "Is that...that...*blood?*" she whispered in horror.

"I've noticed you tend to get kinda white and funny looking whenever you see blood," Holt said. "You have a thing about it, don't you?"

She swallowed. Hard. "Blood makes me faint," she confessed.

"Faint?"

"As in pass out cold."

"Got it. That's not blood."

She gazed up at him trustingly. "It's not?"

"Nope. No way."

"What is it?"

"It's...it's snake ooze."

"Snake ooze?" she asked doubtfully, risking another quick glance. She burrowed into his shirt again. "It's awful red for snake ooze," she said in a muffled voice.

He wrapped his arms around her, holding her tight. "It's red snake ooze," he insisted. "Trust me. I've killed many a snake and they don't bleed. They ooze. There's a big difference."

"I . . . I still feel sort of dizzy."

"Listen up, Tex." He captured her chin and lifted her face to his. He spoke firmly. "Cowboys, *real* cowboys, don't faint at the sight of ooze. Blood, maybe. I've seen it happen on occasion. But never ooze."

She shivered, wanting to believe him . . . desperate to believe him. "No?"

"No."

She relaxed marginally. "It's just that I was so frightened. And Tina . . . Tina!" She looked frantically around. "Where's Tina?"

He rubbed her back with slow, soothing strokes. "She's safe in the ranch house. Everything's fine now. I've got you and everything's going to be all right."

She clutched his shirt, calming beneath his gentle touch. "It's okay? Really okay?" She stared at him, losing herself in his gaze. Something hot and urgent burned in his eyes and her breath caught in her throat. Her grip on his shirt tightened.

"No, Tex. It's not okay," he muttered, his head tilting toward hers. "I don't think it ever was."

Before she had time to react to his harshly spoken statement, Tina's mother descended on them in a flood of grateful tears. The next thing Cami knew, she found herself parted from Holt and knee-deep in guests. As one, they proclaimed her a heroine, shook her hand, slapped her back and passed her around for a group hug.

Gabby approached Holt. "That tears it," he said with a grimace. "Don't suppose we should tell them she killed herself a harmless old bull snake?"

Slowly Holt shook his head. "Best not."

"You do realize this means we'll have to let her stay on. Wouldn't do to fire the fool girl after she's gone and made a hero of herself by beating the stuffing out of a poor defenseless snake."

"No, it wouldn't. Fact is, they'd probably lynch us." A smile crept across Holt's mouth. "Looks like we've got ourselves a new wrangler. She may not be much use with a rope, but she sure has a way with people."

"Not to mention snakes. If'n you was smart, you'd lock up every rope and shovel on the place . . . afore she kills somebody." With that, he stomped off.

Holt waited until the excitement died and the guests had turned their interest to other pursuits before approaching Cami. She peeked at him through shiny black curls, her expression slightly abashed.

More than anything he wanted to sweep her into his arms and kiss her senseless. He wanted to watch those glorious blue eyes deepen with passion, to see that dimpled smile slip across her face, to count each sun-ripened freckle bridging her pert, upturned nose. But most of all, he wanted to toss her across his saddle and take her up into the hills where he could make love to her beneath a star-studded sky, losing himself in her warmth and desire.

But he couldn't. He'd learned that lesson once already. He didn't care to learn it again.

"They sure did make a fuss," she said hesitantly.

He leveled a cool, serious gaze in her direction. "You did good, Tex. You kept your head, you acted instead of panicking and you saved Tina from a potentially dangerous situation."

A swift flush streaked her cheeks. "There wasn't any choice," she insisted in a low, earnest voice.

"Sure there was." Unable to resist, he tucked a stray curl behind her ear. "But it's nice to know I can count on my newest wrangler to act sensibly in times of crisis."

It took a moment for the words to sink in. When they did, he caught the small hitch of her breath right before a huge quavery smile spread across her face. "I'm hired? Permanent for the summer?" He nodded and she launched herself into his arms.

He caught her in a tight embrace. "You're hired, Tex," he confirmed in a husky voice. "Permanent for the summer."

A horn blared behind them and they hastily parted, turning as one. A pale blue Honda glided to a stop, and out of the driver's seat slid one of the most beautiful women Holt had ever seen.

He guessed her to be in her mid-thirties, silky blond hair floating like a silver curtain about a perfect oval face. She was tiny and delicate and wore her pink silk suit, frilly lace blouse and pearls as though born to them. Eyes as blue as a summer sky stared at him, amusement and curiosity gleaming in their depths.

Beside him, Cami started. "Momma," she exclaimed in an astonished voice. "What in the world are you doing *here?*"

CHAPTER SIX

HOLT SHOVED HIS HAT to the back of his head. "Momma?" he repeated in disbelief, looking from Cami to the blonde. "You've got to be kidding."

"No, I'm not kidding," Cami said, pulling her mother into a fierce hug. "This is my momma, Charlotte Greenbush. Momma, this is my boss, Holt Winston."

Holt tipped his hat. "Welcome to the A-OK Corral."

"It's a pleasure, Mr. Winston. And I appreciate your taking such good care of Camellia." Charlotte glanced at her daughter and smiled. "I'm so relieved your two weeks are up. It seems like years since you left Richmond, instead of days."

Cami stirred uneasily. "I've missed you, too." What in the world was going on? Her mother hadn't warned her of a visit, and yet here she stood, big as life. Something had to be up. "Um . . . you didn't mention why you've come. Just passing through?" She couldn't keep the hope from her voice, vain as she knew it to be.

Charlotte laughed. "I've come to bring you home, of course."

Of course. Cami sighed. "Momma," she said, not in the least surprised by her mother's misinterpretation of the facts. "I explained all this to you before I left. I'm working here for the summer."

Her mother clasped her hands together in a white-knuckle grip. "I . . . I assumed that once Mr. Winston realized you didn't know a blessed thing about ranching, he'd send you on your way."

Cami cleared her throat and darted a quick look in Holt's direction. "A reasonable assumption, I'll admit. But he hasn't fired me. Yet."

Holt inclined his head. "Give it time."

Concern lined Charlotte's brow. "In all honesty, I'd rather not give it any more time. I'd hoped that once Camellia had a chance to see how a ranch worked, how different reality is from imagination, she'd be ready to leave." She addressed her daughter, her request softly spoken yet firm. "Why don't you get your things together? We can drive home, just the two of us, and have a nice mother-daughter vacation along the way."

Cami stared at the tips of her boots, struggling to find a tactful way of handling this latest turn of events. Hands down, Charlotte Greenbush was the sweetest momma in the world, a woman who inspired devotion. A kinder, more considerate person had never walked the earth. True, she often seemed a mite helpless. But caring for and pampering her tiny mother came as naturally to Cami as breathing.

For all her twenty-four years she'd tried very hard to grant each of her mother's requests—within reason. Unfortunately Cami couldn't grant this particular one. Being able to work a ranch was important. Too important for giving in.

"Momma, you and I need to get a few things straight," she said, nailing her mother with a cool, unflinching gaze. "All my life, all I ever wanted was to be a cowboy like Poppa. You know that."

"It's a dream," her mother insisted. "A child's fancy."

"I'm not a child any more," Cami said gently. "And being a cowboy's no longer a dream, but an ambition. You have to let go of the old memories and make some new ones."

"Old memories die hard," Charlotte retorted. Her chin wobbled and a sheen of tears misted her eyes. "It's not safe," she whispered. "I lost your father to ranching. I couldn't bear to lose my baby, too."

Regret swept through Cami. But it didn't sway her. She couldn't allow it to sway her. If she didn't hold her ground now, she'd never be able to in the future. "I know you're afraid. But I won't let your fears stop me. It's time I made my own decisions."

Her mother laughed through her tears. "I have no problem with you making your own decisions. So long as your decision is to return to Virginia." At Cami's pointed silence, Charlotte took a step closer. "Please," she implored, offering her hands. "Come home."

Cami closed her eyes, wanting with every ounce of her being to clasp her mother's hands and submit. She could practically feel Charlotte's terror and her love and compassion almost tipped the scales. Almost. Until a picture flowered to life in her mind. Once again she could see her father—raven black hair tumbling across his forehead, hazel eyes aglow with humor and enthusiasm—reaching up and saying, "Come here, Camellia-bush. What a good little cowboy you're gonna make. Daddy's little cowboy."

Slowly she opened her eyes. She couldn't change who or what she was, no matter how much that would hurt her mother. Sure, she'd delayed the inevitable as long as possible. Empathy for Charlotte's fears and memories had kept her close to home far longer than she'd have preferred. But no more. She had to follow her own star. She was a cowboy, through and through. Her decision made, she took a deliberate step back.

"I'm staying." They were the hardest two words she'd ever uttered. She knew how much her decision would hurt her momma. But she couldn't help it.

Charlotte's lips trembled and her hands slowly dropped to her sides. She pulled herself up straight and nodded. "Fine. It's your choice and I respect that. But I'm not leaving until you do."

Cami started in surprise. "Come again?"

"You heard me right. I'm not leaving until you do. When you go, I go. Until then, I'm here to stay."

Cami's mouth fell open. "But... but you can't stay! Only guests and employees allowed. No mothers!"

"Then I'll be a guest," came the obstinate reply. "This is a dude ranch, isn't it?" She looked around for confirmation. "So, make me a dude." With that, she crossed to the car and keyed open the trunk.

"Now, Momma..."

"I'll unload and you can show me where to take my luggage. We'll have a wonderful time together. You can play cowboy and I can keep you safe."

"Good luck," Holt muttered.

Charlotte glanced over her shoulder at Cami. "All you have to do is stay away from cows, horses and sharp instruments. That's not asking too much, is it?"

"Yes!"

"And ropes," added Holt. "You forgot to mention staying away from ropes."

Charlotte blinked. "Really? You have dangerous ropes around here?"

"Only in the hands of certain people." He folded his arms across his chest and gave a significant nod in Cami's direction.

Cool determination settled in Charlotte's blue eyes. "Fine. And no ropes. Aside from that, the sky's the limit."

"Unless you think up any other dangerous activities?" Cami questioned.

"Exactly. We'll still have lots of fun. You'll see."

"Oh, no, we won't see!"

"Sure you will," Holt interjected on an encouraging note. "And once you two are done having fun, you can both go on home to Virginia."

"Exactly!" Charlotte concurred.

"Now wait just one gol'durn minute here." Cami stepped between her mother and the trunk. "Momma, this isn't right. You can't do this. I'm supposed to be working here and you're disrupting that work."

"Now, Camellia..."

"Enough." Her tone brooked no argument. "We had an agreement. You'd allow me to work a ranch for the summer and I'd be home by fall. You gave me your word you wouldn't interfere. Are you going to break your word?"

Charlotte bowed her head, her lips pressed tightly together. "Don't send me away," she whispered in an agonized undertone. "Please, don't."

For an endless moment, mother and daughter faced each other, at an impasse. Then Holt interceded.

"You're in luck, Mrs. Greenbush," he said. "Up until yesterday we were booked solid. But it just so happens we have a two-week cancellation. You're welcome to take over the reservation."

"Two weeks?" Charlotte grabbed at his offer like a lifeline.

He nodded. "We can discuss the possibility of prolonging your stay at the end of that time. Tex?" He shot her a warning look.

"Sounds perfect," she reluctantly agreed, seeing the merits of his suggestion.

She didn't like it. But an ornery stubbornness was one of her mother's less admirable traits. Which meant this might be the only possible solution until Charlotte calmed down and was forced to see sense. Unfortunately, that might take a bit longer than two weeks. More like two years.

Stark relief marked her mother's delicate features. "Thank you so much, Mr. Winston. And please, call me Charlotte."

He held out his hand. "Make it Holt." He glanced at Cami. "I'll put your mother in the blue room at the ranch house. There's a spare bed. You're welcome to stay with her if you'd like."

Stay with her mother? Like a guest? Cami's brows pulled together. Oh, he was smooth. "Come and join your mother," he would offer expansively. "Enjoy your two weeks together. Relax. Have *fun.*" And at the end of Charlotte's visit he'd have them both on their way. She slammed her hat down on her head in perfect imitation of her employer.

"I'm no visiting dude," she informed him. "I sleep with the hands, where I belong."

His expression cooled. "Then snap to it. Help our guest with her luggage."

She nodded grimly. "Yessir, boss. Anything you say."

"OKAY, FOLKS. LISTEN UP." Holt reined Loco to a stop in front of the guests, all mounted on various trail horses. "The next three days away from the ranch are going to be long, action-filled and I hope entertaining. Today we ride to the south pasture where my neighbor and I keep our longhorns. More than two dozen have been hazed down from higher pastureland and need to be rounded up for the drive into Lullabye."

"Are longhorns dangerous?" an older man questioned.

Holt shook his head. "These animals are used for show, so they're familiar with people and pretty docile."

"How do you define docile?" another guest asked dubiously.

Holt sat back in the saddle. "To be honest, I give any animal with six-plus foot of horn plenty of respect and even more maneuvering room. But it takes a bit to rile a longhorn. They're some of the smartest, gentlest cows around."

"Number one rule," Gabby hollered. "Don't rile the longhorns."

Holt waited for the laughter to die before continuing. "It's a good three- or four-hour trip to the pasture with lots of fine scenery between. We'll do some preliminary roundup work today. Afterward, we'll have a hot meal over the camp fire. Believe me when I say, you'll sleep well tonight."

Cami, holding a restless Petunia in check, kept to the far side of Gabby and Frank Smith. She wanted to be close enough so her mother could see her and be reassured, and yet still remain grouped with the other wranglers.

Since the cattle were owned jointly by Holt and Frank, both ranchers had wranglers and guests working the herd in a collective effort. Unfortunately, those who knew what they were doing were somewhat outnumbered by those who didn't...which would make the job that much more difficult.

Holt leaned across his saddle horn, his deep, authoritative voice carrying with ease. "Tomorrow, we round up the last of the stray longhorns and get them situated in the holding pen. Should be a full, hard day's work. There's a cabin nearby, so you'll have the choice of using the bunks there or sleeping on a bedroll under the stars. Friday, we drive the cattle into Lullabye to kick off Western Roundup Days. Any questions?"

A woman raised a tentative hand. "What if... what if it rains?"

A smile drifted across Holt's face. "Why, ma'am, then you'll get wet. Any more questions?" There weren't. "Okay. Let's move out."

By design, each wrangler blended among the guests, chatting casually and answering the unending stream of questions. Holt trotted over to Cami's side.

"How's your mother settling in?" he asked.

Cami tugged the brim of her hat low over her eyes, shading her face from the bright morning sunshine. "Okay, I guess. She's still a bit nervous that I'm going to kill myself."

"With good reason, I'd say."

She ignored him. "Aside from that, she seems to be doing just fine."

"I arranged for Frank to ride with her. Thought it would help take her mind off her only chick."

She peered over her shoulder. Sure enough, Frank Smith rode at her mother's side, engaging her in an animated conversation. They looked good together. Her mother, at forty-three, was a beautiful woman. Yet she'd never remarried, never even had a serious relationship since her husband's death. For the first time, that struck Cami as odd.

She glanced at them speculatively. Frank couldn't be much older than Charlotte, at a guess only a few years. He rode tall in the saddle, a striking man with salt-and-pepper hair and calm gray eyes. Of course, he wasn't anywhere near as striking as Holt. But as a temporary suitor, he'd do.

"Thanks," she said to Holt. "I appreciate your thoughtfulness."

A lazy grin tugged at his mouth. "Frank didn't take much convincing. He seemed happy to help."

As Holt had predicted, the scenery was breathtaking. Cami, content to let the leaders set the pace, chatted with the guests and enjoyed the view. Several hours later, Holt drew up short and waved them in. The guests and wranglers obediently gathered close.

"We're almost to camp," he announced. "As we ride, keep your eyes open for strays. If you see anything, alert one of the wranglers and he'll show you how we round them up. Okay. Fan out and keep your eyes peeled."

Cami winged off to one side of the group, picking her way through brush and rock. She heard the occasional shouts as various members of the group found a stray and herded it in. Gradually, she parted company with the others, intent on finding her own cow. A sudden suspicious movement drew her attention to a mountain mahogany bush. It twitched, rustling in a manner no wind ever created.

She stiffened, excitement blossoming. The distinct possibility existed that a cow made that noise. And if so, this was it! Time to round up them doggies. She brought Petunia's head around and circled the bush. On the far side she found what she sought—a calf.

The calf turned to look at her. A more wicked, mischievous expression, she'd never seen. If she didn't miss her guess, this tyke threatened to be hell on hooves. Fine. She'd find a way to handle hell on hooves. Maybe.

First, she tried to usher the contrary critter toward open pasture. Breaking into a trot, the calf circled the bush and came up behind. She chased him in the opposite direction with similar results. Several more attempts to flush junior from his hiding place ended the same way—the calf the smug winner and Cami the frustrated loser.

Perhaps she should rope it. That was it. She'd show this young maverick who was boss. She unsnapped her rope from the saddle and flipped the loop into the air. Aiming carefully, she tossed it at the wayward animal. At the last possible moment, he ambled forward. The rope snagged in the bush and Cami swore beneath her breath. With a laughing bleat, the calf loped off.

It just figured. She tugged at the rope, but to no avail. And that figured, too, she thought with a sigh.

Clambering off Petunia, Cami fought to free her rope. The bush fought back. With an infuriated cry, she pulled, throwing every ounce of her weight behind the attempt. The rope abruptly jerked loose and she tumbled tin cup over teakettle, before bouncing to a stop on her rump. She winced, rubbing the offending part of her anatomy.

"Dang. That hurts."

As though in response, the bush in front of her rustled ominously. She frowned. What in the world...? Before she had time to gather her wits sufficiently to move, a huge cow head poked through the shrubbery. Oh, lordy! She'd better pray her young maverick had done some mighty fast growing. Because if he hadn't, she was in for major big trouble.

"Junior?" she whispered in a quavering voice. "Is that you?"

In response, a wet, quivering nose drew to within inches of Cami's smaller, drier one. The wet nose inhaled sharply, and for an instant she feared her clothes would be sucked clean off her body.

She let out a squeaky cry of alarm, dug her heels into the dirt and shoved wildly, scooting backward as fast as she could scoot. With an earthshaking bellow, the steer plowed right over the bush after her.

The next thing she knew, the biggest, ugliest, droolingest longhorn she'd ever had the misfortune to meet stood straddled above her, his muzzle hanging an inch from her face. One enormous horn, kinked into more knots than a two-year-old's shoelace, twisted skyward. The other horn, equally contorted, stabbed the ground a yard to her left.

He inhaled again.

She shrieked.

Oh, Lordy, Lordy, Lordy. Don't rile the longhorns, Gabby had said. He'd neglected to mention precisely how one went about avoiding that truly terrible turn of events. She tried to swallow. A powerful thundering reverberated in her ears, growing louder and louder until her whole body shook with it. She pressed a hand to her chest, certain her heart was on the verge of exploding. Any minute now, she'd faint and die horribly.

The thundering subsided, replaced by the crunch of earth beneath boot heel. She risked a quick sidelong glance. "Holt!" she gasped in relief. "Holt, save me!"

"Tex?" He stooped. "That you?"

"It's me, all right."

"Mind telling me what you're doing down there?" he asked in mild surprise.

She cleared her throat. "It's sort of a long story. Maybe I could tell you a bit later?"

"Uh-huh. It can wait. You are aware that layin' flat on your back beneath four thousand pounds of longhorn is not a predicament I'd go out of my way to recommend."

She looked nervously upward. "You understand I'm not in any position to argue with you."

His tone was dry. "That's true enough."

"Holt?"

"Yeah?"

"I don't mean to sound demanding or anything, but do you think you could help me?"

"I'll do my best, but it might prove difficult. Perhaps if I introduced you two...."

"Introduced—"

"Tex meet Buttercup. Buttercup this is Tex."

Buttercup opened his mouth and stuck out the biggest, wettest tongue she'd ever seen. "No," she moaned. "No licking. I don't taste good. Oh, criminy. Don't!"

He did.

"That's disgusting!" she yelped.

Holt grinned. "I think he's taken a shine to you."

She peeked up at the longhorn. To her dismay, she could see a very strange moonstruck expression in Buttercup's eyes. A low, moaning sound rumbled deep in the steer's chest. He threw back his head and bellowed. The ground beneath her shook.

"Holt!"

"All right, calm down." Holt grabbed her beneath the arms and slid her out from under Buttercup.

Gaining her feet, Cami rapidly retreated. Buttercup trotted after her. "Holt, do something!" Holt laughed. "This isn't funny."

"Sure it is. It's springtime and Buttercup's in love. What could be more romantic?" She opened her mouth to retort and he waved her silent. "Maybe he needs to think you're already spoken for."

"Fine." She planted her hands on her hips and faced the steer. "I hate to break this to you, buster, but I'm already spoken for." Buttercup didn't seem the least impressed. With a determined bellow, he stuck out a tongue that threatened another round of slurpy licks and kept coming. Desperate, Cami appealed to Holt. "Don't just stand there!"

Obligingly, he stepped between Cami and the longhorn. "Perhaps a more visual demonstration is in order."

"Say what?"

"A visual demonstration to prove you're spoken for." He swung her into his arms, staring down at her with wicked intent. A wavy lock of sun-kissed hair tumbled across his forehead. "Let's see if he understands this," he said. And covered her mouth with his.

Buttercup and the pasture, the horses and even the Rockies vanished as though they'd never been. All that remained was this man. And he held her—oh, how he held her—in an embrace so close and tight that he controlled the give and take of each breath. His arms formed unbreakable bands about her waist and back, bands she wished could be forged permanently in place. His widespread legs, solid and rooted, trapped her between his thighs as she yielded all will to the mouth that imprisoned hers.

"You think Buttercup has the idea now?" he whispered against her lips.

"Not yet," she whispered back. "Perhaps you should make it a bit clearer."

Complying instantly, he swept off her hat, tossing it onto the grass at their feet. His fingers sank into the tight curls of her hair and he tilted her head to a more accessible angle. Then his hands stroked downward. She trembled beneath the onslaught of his work-roughened touch, trembled as he eased past the fragile bones beneath her throat and dipped into the vee of her shirt.

The buttons fell open beneath his expert management and a startled gasp escaped her. The warmth and fit of his caress felt so right, so natural it didn't occur to her to protest. On the contrary, it took every ounce of willpower to keep from sinking to the ground and allowing nature to take its course.

She wanted this man. Wanted him more than any man she'd ever known...more, she suspected, than any man she ever would know. That knowledge, undeniable and inescapable, terrified her.

A sharp, unexpected nudge knocked them apart and Buttercup released a plaintive moo. It was a long tumble back to reality.

Coming belatedly to her senses, Cami took a hasty step away from pure bliss and fumbled with her shirt buttons. She risked a peek at Holt, a flush mounting her cheeks. At first glance, he appeared unaffected by their encounter. But upon closer inspection, she noted the rapid rise and fall of his chest and the betraying stiffness of his stance.

"For a man with a grudge against city girls, you sure do give them the sweetest kisses," she muttered, picking up her hat and whacking the dust from the brim.

"A temporary aberration."

She lifted her head and met his remote gaze dead on. "Meaning?"

His jaw tightened. "Meaning that in less than two weeks I suspect you'll be returning home with your mother."

She shot him a pitying look. "You suspect wrong. I'll be here for the summer, count on it."

He shrugged. "Two weeks or summer's end, it's still a temporary situation. Knowing that, I don't mind the occasional indulgence."

She felt the first stirring of anger as well as a truckload of hurt. "An occasional indulgence, so long as it doesn't get serious?"

"So long as it doesn't get serious," he confirmed.

She slapped her hat low on her brow. "In that case, I'll stick with Buttercup. At least his affections are sincere."

"I never said my affections weren't sincere."

"Just temporary." At his nod, she stepped back. "No, thanks. I won't be anybody's way station."

"And I won't put my ranch at risk again." His black-eyed gaze hardened. "And you, Tex, are a big risk. You're dangerous. To me. To my ranch. To my way of life."

"Now there you're wrong," Cami dared to say. "*She* was a danger. Not me." Without a backward glance, she snagged Petunia's reins and climbed aboard. "Which way's camp?"

"We'll ride together," he said in a voice that brooked no argument.

Ten minutes later they rode into camp, Buttercup at their heels. Amusement soon replaced the initial shock of having a huge steer tagging behind Cami.

"First time I've ever seen Buttercup bringing up the tail end of a line," Frank commented to Charlotte. "He's our best leader. Sets a good pace. Never balks at anything in his path. Makes moving the herd a hell of a lot easier."

"Best put Tex in front on point," Gabby offered his opinion. "Or we'll never get to Lullabye."

Cami listened to the exchange with interest, wondering why Holt looked less than pleased with Gabby's suggestion. Perhaps he rode point, too, and didn't care for her company. She sighed. If he didn't want her affections, she'd keep them to herself. He'd have nothing to complain about; she'd see to that.

All through dinner and the sing-along that followed, she tried her level best to avoid Holt. Not that that was a problem. He seemed equally intent on avoiding her. And Buttercup did his part, sticking to her side like glue and shoving anyone who came between them from his path. Finally Gabby intervened, leading a pathetically mooing Buttercup off to the holding pen.

As evening deepened, the guests drifted toward the cabin. "You coming, Camellia?" Charlotte asked, standing and collecting a few overlooked pieces of litter.

"Think I'll sleep out here," Cami said, tossing her bedroll by the fire. "I don't often get the chance to sleep under the stars." She frowned. Cute, but a long stretch from the truth. She wanted to sleep here because it was the closest she was likely to get to sleeping with Holt.

Her mother hesitated. "Okay. Sleep well. I'll see you in the morning."

"G'night, Momma," Cami said with a smile.

A few minutes later, Frank stood. "Think I'll turn in, too."

"You gone soft or something?" Gabby asked in disbelief. "Since when do you sleep inside?"

Holt stretched his legs close to the fire. "Since a certain widow lady appeared on the scene. Would that be about right, neighbor?"

Frank grinned, unfazed by their ribbing. "'Bout right," he concurred, and whistling tunelessly he strolled toward the cabin.

Cami nibbled on her lip in concern. She hoped his feelings weren't seriously engaged, since it could only lead to disaster. Her mother would never permit herself to care for a cowpoke again. Her fear of losing another man to ranching would get in the way. If Frank thought he could change her mind, he'd soon learn different . . . sort of like she'd recently learned with Holt. Because Holt Winston would no sooner love a city slicker than her mother would a rancher.

She stewed over the similarities.

When she finally looked up again, she discovered that she, Holt and Gabby were the only ones remaining by the fire. Holt lay propped against his bedroll, his Stetson pulled low over his face. She stared at his hat, overcome with curiosity. Unable to explain why, she reached out to finger the brim.

"Touch that at your peril."

Cami jerked her hand back as though stung. "Why? You have a thing about your hat?" she demanded.

"'Course he does," Gabby spoke up. "A man *is* his hat, Tex. Hell, any cowman worth his salt guards a good Stetson with his life. Fact is, the only time it should leave his head is during the national anthem. And even then I hang tight to mine lest some varmint tries to lift it off me.''

"You don't sleep in it?''

"Dang tootin'. Why, I even shower in it.''

Holt crushed his hat more firmly over his face. "Old man, you talk too much.''

"You see what he just did?'' Gabby queried, completely ignoring his employer.

"You mean the way he squashed it down?''

"That's what I mean, all right. Now you watch next time he does that. Because it speaks to you, loud and clear.''

"Really?'' she asked, fascinated. "What does it say?''

"It says, he's plumb annoyed and intends to be annoyin' in exchange.''

"You might take heed of your own words,'' Holt suggested, one eye peering out from beneath his brim.

"Sure thing. Now. If'n you see him shove that old John B. to the back of his head, why, count on it. He's perplexed, bewildered or surprised.''

Cami smiled, settling more comfortably onto her bedroll. "I take it that doesn't happen often?''

"You take it right.''

"What about when he yanks it low on his forehead like this?'' She demonstrated.

"Why, that means he's aimin' to git what he's aimin' to git.'' Gabby dropped his voice to a hoarse whisper. "But if he ever throws it into the dust—whew-ee, Tex, run for cover!''

"My hat's not the only thing about to eat dust," Holt grumbled. "You going to shut up, or do we need to discuss the matter?"

"Fine thing," Gabby muttered, his mustache bristling. "Fine thing when a man can't express his opinion without bein' threatened with bodily harm." He slouched down on his bedroll, closing his mouth with a snap.

Cami grinned, laying back. For a while she stared at the stars. Then, deciding to work some more on her cowboy skills, she propped her hat to the exact same angle as Holt's. Perfect, was her last thought. Life was perfect.

Within minutes something cold and wet and fuzzy changed her mind. She sat up with a gasp, her hat tumbling off her face and rolling across the ground to land beside Holt. A huge, hulking form hovered over her, so close she could feel its hot, noxious breath on her face.

"Holt!" she shrieked. "Save me!"

CHAPTER SEVEN

HOLT HIT HIS FEET at a dead run, skidded to an abrupt stop and burst out laughing. "Why, Buttercup," he drawled. "It's a little late to come a-courtin', don't you think?"

"Buttercup!" Cami jumped up, relief and amusement replacing her earlier fear. With a sigh, she approached the longhorn and rubbed his nose. "What are you doing here?"

"Musta broke through the fence," Gabby groused. He left his bedroll and grabbed his boots. "Better check the rest of the herd. Probably have one or two escapees to deal with."

"We'll find them in the morning," Holt said. "Tex, see if you can encourage Buttercup to return to his pen while we fix the fence."

Obediently, she gave Buttercup a final rub and crossed to the holding pen. The steer trotted behind. She opened the gate and walked boldly in. Without a murmur of protest, her hulking shadow followed. She latched the gate behind him and climbed onto the fence rail, noting with relief that only one or two longhorns had decided to follow Buttercup's example and vamoose. The rest were settled in for the night.

The huge steer joined her at the rail, blowing warm air into her cupped hand. He nudged her until she gave in and scratched his heavily muscled neck. Beneath the light of a nearly full moon, she made out Gabby and Holt resetting the knocked-down rails, their quiet words and muted grunts drifting to her through the still night air.

She glanced up, amazed by the clarity and brilliance of the heavens. Despite the wash of moonlight, a multitude of stars burned with almost savage radiance, a proper match for the untamed land they crowned. How she loved this place...this life. It fit. Richmond and her former job and friends, in fact everything up until now, seemed like a far distant memory, unreal and undesirable. She belonged here. This land nourished her soul and fulfilled her in a way she instinctively knew to be right and true.

"Beautiful, isn't it?"

She smiled, not in the least surprised by Holt's silent appearance. He, too, belonged. He, too, felt natural and at home. Without him, the dream would be incomplete. "It surely is," she agreed softly. "It's all I hoped it would be. All I ever wanted."

"Enjoy it while you can." His words held a warning. A warning she didn't care to hear. Not now. Not tonight. Not when all about her lay perfection.

"Don't," she whispered. "Don't spoil it."

"It won't last, Tex. Sooner or later you'll have to face that fact."

She bowed her head, squeezing her eyes shut. "No!"

He wrapped an arm around her waist and tipped her backward into his arms. She felt his whipcord strength and power, felt the heat of his body envelop her. He set her on her feet, tucked tight within his hold, pressing her into the taut muscles of his chest and abdomen.

His breath stirred the curls along the curve of her cheek. "This isn't real," he murmured in her ear. "It's the illusion you love, not this life."

"No," she denied fervently. "You're wrong."

He sighed, sending an uncontrollable shiver down the length of her spine. "You're like a young buck, Tex, in love with a fancy lady. You first see her in the evening, when she's at her best, the candlelight and makeup hiding the flaws. And you fall in love with a passion you've never experienced before. But then morning comes and the makeup is washed from her face and sunlight shines through the window, and you see the truth behind the illusion. It's raw and cold and lonely."

"I...I don't understand."

He gripped her chin, forcing her to look at him. The moonlight sculpted his face in hard, remote crags and valleys, and his eyes gleamed with the cold glitter of polished jet. "Ranch life is like that fancy lady." He spoke with a ruthless passion. "You're seeing us at our best, with the grass green and lush and the sun warm against your face. And life is full and rich and rewarding. It isn't always like that."

"I know—"

"You don't know!" He stopped her with a cutting sharpness. "You haven't seen the ranch in the dead of winter when the snow is so deep it's worth your life to leave the safety of the house. Still, you leave because there's livestock counting on you for survival. And the cold, Tex. The cold is so intense it worms into the very marrow of your bones and stays, gnawing at you until you're sick with cabin fever."

"I wouldn't mind! I'd cope. I know I would."

He shook his head. "Maybe the first year you would. But what about the year after and the one after that?

What about when you realize you're trapped and there's nowhere to go, no one to talk to?''

"There'd be you."

The words hung between them. She'd spoken without thinking, and yet she'd spoken the truth. A truth she hadn't been aware of until that very minute. A fierce passion flared in his eyes. His hands tightened on her shoulders and he yanked her closer.

"You're a fool. And I'm an even bigger fool," he muttered. And he kissed her.

He kissed her with a rough passion unlike anything that had gone before. She felt his anger, fierce and unrelenting. And she felt his desolation and pain. She could sense a terrible void in this man. An emptiness that would take an endless supply of love to fill and all the years in a lifetime. She gave him all the love she had, and then gave some more.

Within seconds he broke free, stepping away, his expression closed to her, his body rigid, rejecting all she'd offered.

"Holt?"

"You're riding for a fall, Tex," he informed her in a clipped voice. "If you were smart, you'd get off this particular horse and head home before you break something."

"It's too late for that, I'm afraid," she whispered.

His hands clenched. "So be it. But don't say I didn't warn you." With that, he turned on his heel and stalked away.

Cami stared at his retreating back until the darkness swallowed him. Oh, it was too late all right. Much too late. She'd already taken that fall. And what she'd broken was her heart.

HOLT WAITED UNTIL he heard the crunch of Cami's boots striking out for camp before stepping from the darkness and returning to the holding pen. He leaned against the rail and stared at the cattle, wishing for the first time that he smoked. Better yet, he wished he'd had the foresight to tuck away a flask of something potent and numbing.

Think of the ranch. Think of the men who have fought to carve a place in this country and who have died protecting it. Think of the land. Winston land. My land.

Instead he thought of hair as black as a raven's wing, tumbling in silky ringlets around a face that occupied every moment of his day... and haunted every moment of his nights. He thought of kissing each freckle decorating her pert little nose, and of finding less obvious freckles to kiss. He thought of brilliant blue eyes darkening to navy with the strength of her passion.

And he thought of long winter nights and how they could be spent... with the right woman.

His fist slammed into the fence post, the pain bringing with it a measure of reason and calm. The risk was too great. He couldn't afford to make another mistake. One more like the last and he'd lose everything. He had to decide what was most important.

It was an easy decision. Too bad if it left him with an almost unbearable ache. Aches could be eased. Eventually. They just couldn't be eased by city slickers. There were plenty of women raised on ranches who knew the score. He'd have to find one. He'd have to forget about black hair and dimples and freckles.

He grimaced. Although forgetting those freckles might just about kill him.

THE NEXT DAY CAMI barely had time to think, let alone brood over Holt's remarks. Work began at daybreak with each wrangler teamed with a couple of guests. The different areas around camp were divided among the groups, and the mountains, brush and gullies swept thoroughly for cattle. To her surprise, she enjoyed herself, relaxing and joking with the guests and taking bets to see who could round up the most longhorns.

" 'Fraid I have a bit of bad news," Holt informed them over lunch. "We have a storm on the way. Which means the sooner we've collected and penned the herd, the happier we'll all be. I'd appreciate it if you'd follow the wranglers' directions to the letter. That way we can get the job done as quick as possible and beat that rain."

His announcement set the tone and they didn't waste any time after that. The guests and wranglers worked fast, scouring the surrounding countryside. The afternoon winged by, successful and exhausting, and it was a satisfied if weary band that brought in the final reluctant longhorn.

Over dinner, Cami watched with concern as clouds filled the sky with the heavy threat of rain. As the last bean was scraped from the last tin plate, the heavens opened.

"Haul tail inside!" Gabby shouted, clanging a bell attached to the wall of the cabin. "Frank's got a nice little fire goin' in the hearth and a whole bag of marshmallows just waitin' to be toasted."

Everyone scrambled to collect plates and cups. Laughing at the mad dash, Cami and Charlotte darted beneath the covered porch and stared at the downpour.

"I guess you won't be sleeping under the stars tonight," Charlotte said.

Cami nodded, fighting a stab of regret. "Doesn't look like it."

"I . . . I think you should know something." Hesitating only a moment, Charlotte took a quick breath and rushed on. "I'm actually having a good time. I know it's sort of funny after the fuss I kicked up about your working here and the danger and everything." Her gaze grew distant, as if filled with bittersweet memories. "I guess I'd forgotten how much I enjoyed ranch life."

Cami threw an arm around her mother's shoulders and gave her an understanding hug. "You didn't forget, Momma," she corrected gently.

Charlotte stiffened, releasing a ragged laugh. "You're right. I didn't forget. I put it from my mind. I didn't want to remember, because it was so painful."

"I know," Cami said, compassion welling up inside. "And I understand. You still planning to stay the rest of your two weeks?"

"I'm staying," her mother confirmed.

"And then?"

"And then I guess I learn to let you live your own life." She laughed again, a lighter, freer laugh. "It won't be easy and I don't promise not to interfere every once in a while. But I'll do my best."

Cami grinned. "I love you, Momma."

Her mother grinned back. "I love you, too, Camellia."

The door opened behind them and Frank appeared. "Come in and join the sing-along, Charlie," he suggested, drawing Charlotte off. "You've got the prettiest voice here. It would be a darned shame to let it go to waste."

She glanced over her shoulder—a quick bonding mother-daughter sort of look—before linking arms with Frank. "Why, thank you, kind sir. Don't mind if I do."

They entered the cabin, leaving Cami alone with her thoughts. Her mother had finally found a small portion of happiness and peace of mind. Cami sighed. If only she could find a similar peace... one she could share with Holt. She gazed out at the rain falling in a steady gray sheet.

Her mouth curved in a wistful smile. *Give it up.* No sense in wishing for the impossible. Some things were never meant to be. She turned toward the light and laughter. Opening the door to the cabin, she abandoned the chilly solitude of hopeless wishing for the certainty of warmth and companionship.

HOLT STIRRED FROM HIS stance at the far end of the porch, fighting the urge to catch Cami before she disappeared inside. He wanted to run with her into the rain-drenched night and find a private spot where they could be alone, where he could indulge their passion and sate the craving gnawing at his gut.

His mouth curved in a self-deprecatory smile. *Give it up.* No sense in wishing for the impossible. Some things were never meant to be. He turned from the light and laughter. Stepping from the porch, he abandoned the possibility of warmth and companionship for the chilly solitude of a purging rain.

CAMI AWOKE ABRUPTLY AND rolled over in her bunk bed, not quite sure what had disturbed her sleep. It came again—a pounding outside the cabin that brought her to full and startled consciousness. It wasn't the pounding of rain on the tin roof, although she could hear that, too. Nor was it a person pounding on the door. No, this was a loud, insistent banging.

Moooo.

With a groan, she buried her face in the pillow. She'd know that moo anywhere. Buttercup. She jumped to her feet, dressing as quickly and quietly as she could so as not to disturb the other women, and ran from the room. She slammed dead on into Holt.

"You heard him, too?" he asked. At her nod, he muttered, "Damned cow."

Together they crossed to the front door and flung it open. Buttercup stood on the porch blinking at them. He took one look at Cami, released a desperate bellow and tried to push his way into the cabin. Holt hurled himself against the steer, throwing every ounce of weight into a vain attempt to stop the animal from gaining entrance.

"Haul butt outside, Tex!" he yelled, as he rapidly yielded ground to the determined longhorn. "Frank, Gabby, get out here. Fast!"

Cami slipped past, calling to the lovesick steer. An instant later the two men showed up, Gabby in bright red long johns. "What's Buttercup doin' in our cabin?" he demanded.

"How the hell should I know? Probably busted out of the holding pen again. Tex! Get him off the porch before he annihilates the place."

"If he broke loose..." Frank began.

"—then the other longhorns will follow suit and head for the hills," Holt confirmed.

Gabby slapped on his hat. "Let's go get us some cows."

"Why tonight?" Cami called. "It's so dark and rainy, we'll never find them."

Holt spared her a brief glance. "We're out of time. If we don't get them now, there isn't going to be a cattle drive through town tomorrow. This rain will quit soon, and there's a full moon tonight. Once the clouds pass we'll see just fine." He yanked at the brim of his Stetson. "I hope."

"I'll gather my boys and head west as far as Blackman's Ridge and south to Deadman's Gulch," Frank said. "You want to cover the east ridge, Gabby?"

"Soon as I find my britches."

"Tex and I'll fix the holding pen and get Buttercup settled," Holt decided. "Once we're done, we'll ride north. Meet here by daybreak and we'll see how we stand." With that, they scattered.

Cami quickly discovered that repairing a holding pen in the pouring rain was wet and muddy work and even less of a pleasure than she'd expected it would be. By the time they'd finished, they were both filthy. "What do we do about Buttercup?" she asked in concern. "If we put him back in the pen, he'll only bust loose again."

Holt dropped the last rail in place and wiped his brow with a mud-encrusted sleeve. "His little infatuation hasn't left me much choice. We'll have to snub him." He caught her sudden frown. "It won't hurt," he reassured. "We'll tie him head-on to a tree, is all. And it won't be for long."

Just as they got Buttercup settled, the rain slackened and a bright, full moon appeared from behind the rapidly scattering clouds. They saddled their horses and started north, fanning out but staying within shouting distance. As the hours wore on and they didn't find a single cow, Cami grew more and more discouraged.

Breaching a steep ridge, she came across Holt. He sat on Loco, unmoving, staring up at the night sky. She reined in her horse, reluctant to approach, yet drawn by the bleakness of his expression, by the urge to comfort.

"Tex?" He spoke without turning around.

"It's me, all right. How'd you know I wasn't a cow?"

"I just knew." He turned and to her amazement, a smile eased the hard lines of his face. "You're filthy."

She grinned back at him. "I'm filthy? Check a mirror, buckaroo. You look like a mud slick with eyeballs."

"A mud slick with eyeballs. Great." He hesitated, apparently fighting some inner quandary. She knew the moment he came to a decision, for he stiffened his spine and glanced at her, his gaze resolute. "I have a solution, if you're game."

It didn't take much thought. "I'm game."

"Come on. There aren't any cows to be found here."

They rode in silence through the woods, the moon lighting their path. Cami didn't speak, afraid she'd break the mood. And it was a good mood—companionable, comfortable, relaxed. They angled to the northeast and plunged into a dense stand of pines. Shrubs snagged her jeans and made the going difficult.

"Not much further," he said, urging Loco through the thick brush.

Over a final hill, they emerged from the woods into a clearing and Cami stared in wonder. Trees and bushes circled the hidden glade forming a seemingly unbroken hedge. Thick green grass began where the woods ended, moss-covered rocks and clumps of ferns dotting the landscape. And smack-dab in the center was a pool, steam rising from the center.

"What? How?" Cami stammered.

"Hot springs. They're all through the Rockies. I found this one a number of years back and kept its location to myself.'' He glanced her way, his expression obscured by shadows. ''Until now.''

She caught her breath, not mistaking his meaning. A fierce wave of heat swept through her. ''Holt...''

He swung off Loco. ''Care to join me?''

''Yes.''

''Then climb down and tie your horse to a breeze.''

''Don't mind if I do,'' she said gruffly and dismounted.

Wisps of steam rose from the water, creeping across the surrounding terrain and clinging to the foliage with ghostly fingers. Holt sat on a large rock at one end of the pool and tugged off his boots, tossing them aside.

''It's the best hot bath you'll ever have. And there's the added advantage of rinsing off some of this mud.''

She followed his example and shed her boots. Awkward, she lingered by the pool. Holt showed no such hesitancy. Clamping his hat to his head, he dropped into the water.

''Is it... is it very hot?'' she asked.

''Nope. Just right. A few of the springs I've found will boil the skin clean off your bones. This one's a shade warmer than bathwater. Hot enough to ease an achy muscle, but not so hot you end up like a lobster.''

''Sounds nice.'' She bit down on her lip, peeping across the steaming water at him.

''It feels nice, too.'' His voice had deepened, turning rough and raspy. He looked directly at her, holding her with a clear, compelling stare. ''Come here.''

Instinct made her pause, alert to the predatory nature of his command, acutely aware that he was the hunter, she the prey. But an irresistible allure drew her, compelled her to submit to his demand, to yield to his power and strength. Without a word, she slid into the water.

Delicious heat enveloped her and her eyelids fell shut. She sighed, feeling each muscle as it relaxed, the tension melting away as though it had never been. A series of ripples lapped across her shoulders and she opened her eyes, snared by the intensity of Holt's gaze. He drifted nearer, crowding her, corralling her, closing off any chance of escape. Not that she wanted to escape.

"Good?" he murmured.

She nodded. "Great."

He slipped off her hat and sent it spinning across the glade. His followed a moment later. Moonlight danced in his sun-streaked hair, transforming the gold to silver. But it was his expression that held her attention. There she read his desire, desire that carved deep furrows beside his mouth and left its mark in his black glittering eyes.

"Grab some air," he warned, before pulling her beneath the water.

She didn't struggle. She knew he wouldn't harm her. His hands moved up and into her hair, swishing the dirt from her curls. An instant later, he kicked for the surface.

"Better?"

She clung to him, laughing. "Much. I don't suppose you have any shampoo?"

"'Fraid not." He cupped her face. "Tex..."

She smiled up at him. "What?"

"I'm going to kiss you now."

Her smile slowly faded and an incontrollable trembling began. She licked her lips, her eyes drifting closed. "Yessir, boss. Anything you say," she whispered.

She felt his breath against her face. Gently, so very gently, his mouth touched hers, drinking the moisture from her parted lips. She tasted the slightly metallic tang of the pool... and then she tasted him, as intoxicating as fine wine. She wound her arms around his neck, surrendering to his fierce kisses.

Control slid away and with it any thought of resistance. Even when he unbuttoned her shirt, ridding her of the irritating drag of wet cotton, she didn't resist. She welcomed the lightness, the unaccustomed freedom.

His hands encircled her waist, the calluses ridging his fingertips scraping the sensitive skin of her abdomen. His mouth left hers, sliding downward, dipping into the hollow of her throat before seeking the fullness of her breasts.

She shuddered, crying out the only word her shattered mind could summon. "Holt!"

For an instant time froze. And in that frozen instant she realized that she loved this man. Completely, totally and forever.

Holt pulled back, the sound of his name returning to him a measure of rational thought. He fought for breath...hell, fought for even a smidgen of control. He didn't dare kiss her again. If he did, he'd take her and to hell with the consequences. It would be all too easy to lose himself in her warmth and sweetness and passion. Gritting his teeth, he encircled her waist and lifted her onto the rim of the pool.

"Strip off your jeans." She started to argue, but he interrupted with crisp authority. "Wring them out and lay them on the rock to dry. I'll hand you mine."

"I don't mind wet jeans," she protested, shivering beneath the mild breeze stirring the surrounding pines.

A cynical smile touched his mouth. So, modesty had returned. From long experience he knew regret wouldn't be far behind. "Bull. Don't turn bashful on me, Tex. I'm not suggesting we go skinny-dipping. I won't even touch you, if that's what you'd prefer. I just want to give our clothes a chance to dry. Riding wet is not my idea of fun."

She hesitated, then gave in. He watched as she struggled free of her soaked jeans. As far as he could tell the only difference between her briefs and most swimsuits was that her briefs revealed less skin. What they did reveal, though, were her long, slender legs. He closed his hands into fists to keep himself from snagging one of those dainty little ankles and yanking her back into the water. Back into his arms where she didn't belong.

He passed her his clothing and struck out across the pool to retrieve her shirt. He threw it to her and she arranged the wet clothes on the rock before returning to the water. But he noticed she kept her distance.

"Having second thoughts?" he asked.

"One or two," she admitted. "It's not unreasonable, when you consider...everything."

"Not unreasonable at all."

"Holt?"

"What is it, Tex?"

"Tell me what she did. Tell me how she ended any hope for a future with you." The words echoed across the pool.

The pain and disillusionment in her voice caught him square in the gut. He turned and looked at her through the steam. Beaded water dripped from her curls to round white shoulders, the drops sparkling like scattered diamonds in the moonlight. Finally he spoke. "I met Leigh in Dallas."

"She was a Texan?" Cami said with a disbelieving gasp.

"That surprise you?"

"I think so." She tilted her head to one side. "I have to admit, it does. It surely does."

"Why? Because you're a Texan?" He didn't wait for her to respond, he knew the answer. "Sort of kills your theory, doesn't it? Not all Texans are born cowboys."

Cami shot him a familiar defiant look. "Her genes must have mutated. It happens every once in a while. You probably picked one of the few women in the whole state of Texas not born to be a cowboy."

"Right." His sarcasm made her wince. "Anyway, it was springtime. We fell in love. I married her and brought her home. It was all very fast. Very romantic."

"And what happened?"

"Nothing at first. She settled into ranch life. Or at least her idea of ranch life."

"Which was?"

"Playing lady of the manor. Agnes took care of the house. I took care of the stock."

"And Leigh?"

"She took care of herself." He closed the distance between them. "Winter arrived. Leigh left."

Cami frowned. "That's it? That's all? End of story?"

He ground his teeth at her nonchalant attitude. "One small codicil. She did manage to clean out my savings on her way through the door."

"Let me get this straight. You fell in love with the wrong woman and because of that you're not willing to give..."

She broke off, momentarily flustered, and he wondered what she'd been about to say. "Us?" he suggested. A deep flush streaked her cheekbones and he knew he'd guessed right.

"...*romance* another try," she corrected doggedly.

"Wrong. I fell in love with a city girl and learned a few important lessons as a result. One. City girls can't handle ranch life. And two. Don't bet the ranch on a losing hand."

She hit the pool with her fist, spraying him with water. "You are plumb loco, Holt Winston. If Leigh truly loved you, she'd never have left. In fact, she would have adored wintertime."

That gave him pause. "Oh, yeah? And why is that?"

"Because," she said without hesitation. "Because she would have had you all to herself. Things slow down a bit in winter, don't they? No roundups, no dawn-to-dusk days, no distractions. Just you and a roaring fire and...and..." Her voice trailed off and she bit her lip, as if aware she'd said too much. Far too much.

He drifted closer. "And?"

"Don't," she whispered. "Please don't tease me."

"Tease you!" he exclaimed. "You drive me crazy, you know that? I won't breathe easy until you've high-tailed it off my ranch and are back in Richmond where you belong."

She shook her head. "I don't belong there."

"You don't belong here." He caught her in his arms. "I should never have brought you to this place." She looked at him with those heavenly blue eyes and desire ripped through him with the elemental force of a killer tornado.

"But you did. Why?"

"So I could do this." He dipped his head and kissed her with an urgency he couldn't conceal. He wanted her. And he made sure she knew it.

She eased back and peered up into his face with a sweetly earnest expression. "I'm not like Leigh," she attempted to reassure him. "One of these days you'll realize that."

He froze. He needed the reminder. It was probably the only thing that saved her. He couldn't take, not unless he gave something in exchange. It wouldn't be right. And he had nothing to give her. Forcibly, he set her from him. "Not today I won't."

"Holt..."

"Get out of here, while I can still let you. 'Cause what's gonna happen if you stay may relieve my ache, but it won't change a thing between us."

He saw her illusions shatter, saw the loss of hope and trust and innocence. And he, bastard that he was, did nothing to stop it.

She didn't wait for another invitation. She shot out of the water and snatched her clothes from the rock. Struggling into her damp jeans and shirt, she raced over to Petunia. She mounted and turned to look at Holt.

For a long moment, their gazes met. With a shrill "Hiyah," she wheeled her horse and tore from the glade as if the devil himself were at her heels.

CHAPTER EIGHT

CAMI MANAGED TO SNATCH a few hours of sleep before daylight. Crawling from bed and facing the morning sun, though, proved almost more than she could handle. Until she discovered she was the last one up.

Tossing on her clothes, she raced outside. All the wranglers and guests stood in a group around Holt, Gabby and Frank, intent on a serious discussion. She crept closer, hoping to listen in without drawing attention her way.

"I don't think it's wise to divide up the group," she heard Holt say.

"I'm not talking about dividing the group," Frank insisted. "There are only four longhorns still missing. I need one volunteer to help find them. We'll be a couple hours behind you at most."

"I'll still be two men short working the herd," Holt made the point.

Frank stared at the ground, his patience clearly running out. "You know these animals aren't going to give you any grief. You have more than enough wranglers to move them. Two men more or less won't amount to a hill of beans."

To Cami's utter astonishment, her mother spoke up. "I'll help Frank."

"Now, Charlie," Frank began.

Charlotte smiled, her expression wryly amused. "I know. I seem like some helpless city girl, right? Well, I'm not. I lived on a ranch for a few years and worked roundup with my husband. I know my way around cattle well enough to bring in four strays."

Holt's eyes narrowed and he glanced from Frank to Charlotte. "Okay. You two start out now. Everyone else, pay attention to your assigned positions." He ran through the roster until he reached Cami's name. He looked up, his arctic black gaze colliding with hers and she knew that last night might never have been. "Glad you could make it, Tex," he said coolly. "You're on flank."

"Thought you wanted her on point so she could be at lead with Buttercup," Gabby reminded him.

"You thought wrong," Holt snapped. "We're a couple men short, remember? I don't have the manpower to spare two at point."

"But, Buttercup..."

Holt's jaw tightened. "I'll keep Buttercup in line. I don't plan on spillin' the herd just because our lead steer has gone and got himself a crush on one of my hands. Tex, you're on flank."

She squashed her hat low on her brow. If that's the way he preferred to play it, that's the way she'd play it. "Yessir, boss."

He addressed the guests. "We're in for fun and plenty of it. The main rule is to keep to your assigned positions. Those behind me on swing will be responsible for holding the cattle in line. Remember though, keep what you've got. If you have a cow take off, let those in the rear bring 'em back home. That's what flank and drag are for."

"When we're not eating dust, you mean?" one of the guests hollered.

Holt inclined his head. "When you're not eating dust. Any more questions?" There weren't. "Okay. Let's mount up and move out. We're due in Lullabye in four hours."

Gabby released the cattle from the holding pen in a long string, Buttercup leading the way, Holt not far behind. Four of Frank's men fell into swing. Several cows later, Cami and several guests took their positions at flank. Gabby and the remaining guests moved in behind the herd at drag.

As Holt had predicted, they kept busy. The cattle were at their most difficult, determined to go in the exact opposite direction of where they were driven. Three hours later, Cami could barely contain her exhaustion. The sleepless night, the kisses she'd shared with Holt...and their rather distressing conversation, all took a toll. And she still had another hour of hard riding.

Gritting her teeth, she cut off an escapee and circled the cow back into the herd. "Cut the nonsense, Tulip," she scolded. "You owe me for saving you from that rope-happy city slicker. Now behave yourself or I'll turn him loose on you again."

Tulip obediently rejoined the herd and Cami nodded in satisfaction. She could do this. After all, she'd waited her entire life for an opportunity to work on a ranch. It was cowboy work. It was her first love.

Her first love next to Holt.

She caught her breath at the unwelcome reminder, choking on a mouthful of dust. Misery welled through her and she stared at Holt's back, swaying in the saddle as though one with the horse, moving with a natural rhythm she could only envy. She'd never shied from the truth before and she wouldn't now. She loved the man. For all the good it did her. For all he cared.

And yet deep in her heart she suspected he did care. Despite all that had happened, all he'd said, he felt something. And perhaps that was enough...if she could work past his prejudice against city slickers. *And Texas women!*

"Heads up!" the command floated back. "Lullabye's just over the next ridge."

Relief flowed through Cami. Not much further now. Drive them straight down Main Street and into the corral. What could be simpler?

What indeed.

It didn't happen until they were three-quarters of the way through the center of town. A little boy, no more than five, darted into the street. Swaggering up to Tulip, he tugged his toy cap gun from his miniature holster and pulled the trigger.

All hell broke loose.

Tulip—already on the spooked side due to the masses of people lining the street, cheering and hollering and carrying on—took exception to the boy's actions. With a trumpetlike bellow, she charged him. The child's father, recognizing the possible ramifications of two thousand pounds fixing to mow them down, snatched up his son by the seat of his pants and took off at a dead run. Fortunately for Cami's peace of mind, most of the nearby crowd also recognized imminent disaster when they saw it and scattered.

The cow, set firmly on her course and resembling nothing so much as a locomotive on a fast track to tomorrow, crashed through the rail lining the boardwalk. Like lemmings heading for the sea, a half-dozen others followed her lead, Cami on their collective tails, clinging to the pommel and hollering loud enough to wake the dead.

All but Tulip found their way back to the main herd with some able assistance from Gabby. With unswerving determination and a true talent for destruction, Tulip continued along her path of ruin, smashing everything within horn's reach. Down the boardwalk she went, Cami in hot pursuit.

Reaching Lem's Mercantile and General Gathering Spot, Tulip bounded over a sack of grain and crashed through the front door. Petunia, ever valiant and faithful in her duly appointed job as cow fetcher, followed right behind.

"Coming through," Cami had the presence of mind to shout.

Lem leapt onto the counter and wrapped his arms around the cash register. His son, Lorin, dove into the frozen-food case and burrowed beneath the chocolate-chocolate fudge and raspberry-swirl parfait ice cream. His wife, Carlene, scampered nimbly up the wall shelves lined with preserves, jellies and pickled beets. Jars smashed to the ground.

The cow plowed down a row of groceries, her horns ripping through bags, sacks and plastic. Flour filled the air. Sugar, salt and various spices scattered across the floor, making the going underfoot treacherous. Until, that was, the longhorn knocked over the display of cooking oil and molasses. Then the going underfoot was gone.

Petunia slid down the aisle on her rump, Cami gamely clinging to the saddle.

Finished with the first aisle, Tulip picked up speed and tackled the canned foods. Like a giant can opener, she ripped through tins of tomatoes, creamed corn and soups. She rounded the next corner and barreled full steam down the preserve aisle. The assortment of fruits already splattered across the floor made for a slippery, if colorful runway.

Tulip hit it flat out.

She took off like a jet-propelled bullet. The only thing that kept her from breaking the sound barrier was Lem's south wall. A huge mural covered that wall depicting the gold rush of '49. She rammed it with such force that Lem found himself with a second rear door smashed right through a miner's stomach.

The last Cami saw of Tulip she was headed south, a chunk of wood inscribed with "California or Bust" stuck to her horns. For generations to come, stories from as far away as Mexico would drift back to Lullabye of a strange crazed longhorn still running as though the devil himself were at her heels.

The dust settled.

Cami, seated atop Petunia, slowly surveyed Lem's Mercantile and General Gathering Spot. Or rather, what remained of Lem's Mercantile and General Gathering Spot. Row after row of ruin and desolation lay scattered about her. Flour hung thick in the air, covering everything with a dense white blanket. Petunia sneezed. Cami followed suit.

Lem hopped off the register. Carlene clambered down from the shelving. Lorin peeked out of the frozen-food case.

"What in the *hell* happened?" A voice broke the shocked silence. It was a deep, furious and painfully familiar voice.

She didn't dare look around. "That you, Holt?"

"Good guess. You okay, Tex?"

"Fine and dandy." She risked a quick peek over her shoulder. "I bet you wish you'd put me on point, right?"

He didn't respond, but his eyes began to burn like wildfire. That gave her pause. "You sure you're okay?" He spoke slowly. Distinctly. With great care.

"Positive."

"Good. Get ... off ... that ... horse."

"Now, Holt, don't be mad at Petunia. She was only doing her job."

"Get ... off ... that ... horse ... now!"

"You see, Tulip—"

"Get off the fool horse, woman!"

She tumbled off Petunia. "It was that darn kid. He shot Tulip and Tulip didn't take kindly to it. She jumped the rail and ... and ..." Something about his expression had her backing up, slipping and sliding through a mixture of salt and sugar, oil and molasses. Holt slipped and slid after her.

"You were supposed to head the cows off at the pass, Tex," he said through gritted teeth. His hands clenched and unclenched at his sides.

She nodded frantically. "By golly, you're right. I was. That old cow got the jump on me, I admit it."

Lem came up behind Holt and grabbed his arm. "Now, Holt, take it easy. These things happen. At least, I'm pretty sure they do."

Holt shook off the store owner. "Not with my wranglers they don't."

"Even the best of them can make a mistake now and then," Lem tried again. "Why, remember Willy Hawkin's cattle drive? His cows made off with a whole rack of Trudy's feminine fripperies."

Holt swiveled, staring at Lem in disbelief. "You're defending her? After what happened to your store? Just look at this place!"

Lem shook his head. "Tex taught our boy, Lorin, the most amazing yo-yo tricks you ever did see. Spent hours with him. Showed more patience than any of those special-ed teachers he's got. We're mighty fond of her." He glanced around and cleared his throat, his voice a bit fainter. "Mighty fond."

Cami struggled to retain her balance amid the oil slick beneath her boots. "Why, thanks, Lem. That's darn neighborly of you. Tell you what. Let me get Petunia out of here and I'll be right back. Why, with a bit of elbow grease..." she surveyed the damage and gulped "...or maybe a *lot* of elbow grease, we'll have your store set to rights in no time."

Townspeople began to poke their heads in the front door.

"That's the spirit, Tex," Reverend Sam said from the shattered remains of the doorway. "We'll all help. And we'll take up a collection to cover anything the insurance doesn't."

"Now wait just one cotton-pickin' minute," Holt began.

"Don't you feel bad, Tex," Wes interrupted. "It could have happened to any one of us." He thought it over. "If we had longhorn cattle. And if we ran 'em through town. And if we put a complete novice on flank." He cleared his throat. "How 'bout I run home and grab my hammer and nails. Once we're done here, we can all head over to my soda shop for ice cream. My treat."

"You can't give her ice cream. I'm not done slaughtering her yet!"

"And my boy has a few pine boards we can use to replace those shelves," Clara called. "It's the least we can do, considering how Tex helped Darryl when he sprained his ankle so bad. Bandaged him up slick as you please."

A portly man jumped across a jumble of minestrone soup cans and offered his hand. "Tommy Torrino. I'm the mayor of this fine town. Sorry I missed you last time you were here." He addressed the crowd. "What do you say, folks? Shall we all pitch in?" A collective cheer rang out.

Cami looked around, a sheen of tears misting her eyes. "Thanks," she said. "This sure is one special town."

Holt took a deep breath and surrendered to the inevitable. "Somebody have a spare broom? Time's a-wastin'. We have a dance to get to, and a whole lot of store to clean."

CAMI STOOD, HANDS ON her hips, in the guest room her mother occupied at the ranch. "Of course you have to go to the dance, Momma. I told everyone you'd come. You wouldn't want to make a liar out of me, would you?"

Her mother shook her head, her face white and strained. "I'd really rather not, Camellia."

"But you love dances. And I've put a dress on and everything." Cami smoothed the bright rose skirt self-consciously, dropping to the bed beside her mother. "What's wrong?"

Charlotte clasped her trembling fingers together, avoiding Cami's eyes. "I'm thinking of returning home."

"Returning home!" Cami frowned. "But yesterday you were so happy, so reconciled to the past and ranches and the cowboy way of life. What..." She broke off, bewildered. "Tell me what's going on."

"I guess I'm shaken by what happened today."

"At Lem's?" she asked doubtfully, something in her mother's voice not ringing quite true.

Charlotte nodded. "I know you weren't in any real danger and I know you weren't hurt. I...I just think it's best if I went home."

"Before the dance." Cami tilted her head to one side. "That doesn't make a bit of sense and you know it. Are you positive there isn't anything else?"

Her mother smiled brightly. "What else could there be?"

"I can't imagine. Especially since I know my mother has always been open and honest and forthright. So you couldn't possibly be hiding anything." She shot her mother a searching glance. "Right?"

Charlotte stirred. "Camellia..."

"And since tomorrow is the earliest you can leave, that gives us all the time in the world for the dance tonight." She stood and pulled her mother to her feet. "Not another word. You're going and that's all there is to it."

"You don't understand," her mother moaned in despair.

"Nope, I surely don't. Care to explain what's really bothering you?"

"It's nothing." She gazed at her daughter, an almost frantic quality to her expression. "You look so much like your father. The same black hair, the same wide smile. I loved him. You know that, don't you?"

Cami's voice softened. "Of course, I do. I figured out long ago that you two shared a once-in-a-lifetime love affair."

For a minute her mother seemed on the verge of saying something. Then she shook her head. "Never mind," she murmured, her shoulders drooping. "I'll go to the dance."

Cami hesitated, but knew she wouldn't get any more information tonight. She linked arms with her mother. "That's the spirit. Come on or we'll be late."

Two station wagons waited outside to transport the guests into town for the Western Roundup dance. Thirty minutes later, they arrived at the hall to find the party in full swing. From the minute she walked in the door, Cami found herself besieged by dance offers. Accepting Wes's hand, she checked over his shoulder to be sure her mother didn't lack a partner. To her relief Frank stood by Charlotte's side, coaxing her onto the floor.

The time flew by, Cami moving from one partner to the next, but never once dancing with the man she wanted to more than anyone else. He didn't approach until toward the end of the evening. He waylaid her by the punch bowl. Without a word, he took the glass of Trudy's "Hawaiian surprise" from her hand and led her onto the dance floor.

Cami melted into his arms and they danced. His hand, planted low on her back, caressed her spine. His intent black gaze held hers, never once drifting as he swung her around and around the oak floor. She didn't hear anything, feel anything, except the brush of his hard thighs against her legs and his broad chest rising and falling in perfect tempo with her own.

When the music drew to a close, he ushered her through the open doors and into the darkness outside.

They weren't the only couple to seek the moonlight. But Holt clasped her hand and led her away from the hall, until the music and laughter were a mere whisper on the night breeze.

He fingered the thin strap of her rose-colored dress. "You look beautiful tonight."

"You look rather handsome yourself," she admitted, admiring the way his shoulders filled his dress shirt. She stared at him, struggling to read his thoughts, wishing she had the nerve to make the first move and throw herself into his arms.

As if reading her mind, he tugged her closer. "I've been wanting to do this all evening," he said, and kissed her.

Beneath his touch all differences seemed to melt away as if they'd never been. Held tight in his arms, anything seemed possible. City slickers could become cowboys and a stubborn rancher could love another Texas woman. A ranch house could become a permanent home filled with love and laughter and the patter of tiny cowboy feet.

Eventually they surfaced for air. For a long time neither spoke. She could have spent the rest of the night nestled in his arms. But she suspected there were one or two issues they should address.

"I'm sorry about Lem's store," she said, breaking the silence between them.

A muscle leapt in his jaw. "You pitched in to set it to rights. Lem appreciated that."

"Everyone helped. Even you." She peeked up at him. "It all worked out in the end, didn't it?"

A frown gathered between his brows. "His store will recover, and eventually Lem will, too. But that's not the point."

He seemed to check himself, cut off the words she sensed raging within. "We never did have a chance to clear the air," she prompted. "I suppose this is as good a time as any. Unless you don't want to?" She tried not to look too hopeful.

He took a deep breath, foolishly taking her at her word. "Today was bad, Tex. I admit, it could have been worse. But it never should have happened. A cowboy who knows his business would have prevented that longhorn from ever getting into Lem's store."

"I admit my cowboy instincts let me down this time."

Anger flared. "That's enough, Tex. Face facts. You don't have any cowboy instincts to let you down, because there's no such thing. You learn this business by doin' it, day after day, month after month, year after year. It isn't a talent you're born with, it isn't encoded in your DNA at conception. It's a job with skills that have to be learned."

"I'm learning. I am!"

He turned slightly away. "That's a matter of opinion. If nothing else, today should have taught you just how limited your skills are. Take it as a warning. Don't get cocky. And stop telling yourself that you're a natural-born cowboy. It'll only lead to disaster."

She met his gaze with cool defiance. "I guess we'll have to agree to disagree on this particular topic. I am a cowboy where it counts—in my heart. And I always will be."

She turned to leave, but he caught her arm in an iron grip. "Go home. Before you get hurt."

She didn't look at him, merely shook her head. With an exclamation of fury, he spun her around. "You drive me crazy, woman." He snatched her in his arms and planted a hard, passionate kiss on her mouth. Then he set her from him. "You're about as safe to my peace of mind as a busted railroad crossing. Let's get back inside, before we do something I'll regret."

CAMI QUICKLY FOUND THAT after Western Roundup, the ranch swung into full action. The next two weeks passed with astonishing speed. The days were long and difficult... and the most marvelous she'd ever experienced. There were herds to be rounded up, bulls to be scattered and yearlings gathered for shipment. Determined to prove her worth to Holt, she worked harder than she ever had in her life.

To her surprise Charlotte continued to linger, and Holt continued to find room for her at the ranch. And though her mother never interfered with Cami's duties, she seemed edgy and anxious.

"Leave her be," Frank recommended. "What she's facing she has to face alone. There's nothing you can do to help."

"I don't understand," Cami complained.

Frank hesitated. "I think it has to do with being back on a ranch."

Dismay filled her. "I know, but... If it's so painful, why doesn't she just leave?"

"She knows it's time to overcome her fears...or give in to them." His gray eyes grew bleak. "Let's hope it's the one, and not the other."

Cami's concern deepened. Was she to blame? Did her mother stay—and suffer—because of her? If so, she'd soon put a stop to it. Before she could take action, Holt called her over. He and several of the guests stood near the corral.

"Time to get to work," he announced. "Today, we get to see how well you folks can rope."

Cami groaned. For some reason she still hadn't found her rope user friendly, and most everyone knew it. "You want me to watch, right?" she suggested. The guests laughed. Even Holt laughed, something he hadn't done for a while.

"Nope. I want you in there with the rest of them, Tex. Y'all are going to experience firsthand the fine art of wrasslin'. That herd of Herefords we rounded up need to be branded and vaccinated and checked for injury."

"We're ... we're not going to brand them ourselves, are we?" one woman asked in a faint voice.

Cami gulped. Just how much of that red oozy stuff was involved in branding and vaccinating? she wondered uneasily.

"Gabby will be doing the branding," Holt assured them, much to Cami's relief. "Okay. This is how it works. I'm going to split you into two teams. The first team ropes the calf and drags him out. The second team grabs the critter, flips and holds him down while he's branded and vaccinated. Tex, get Petunia into the corral and let's see what you can do."

"Petunia's not a cuttin' horse," Gabby said to Holt.

"No, but she'll put up with our wrangler's antics better than any other horse I have. So today, Petunia's a cutting horse."

Self-consciously, Cami saddled Petunia and entered the corral. She noticed her mother coming to stand at the rail to watch. Cattle milled at one end. Slowly she rode to the edge of the herd, picking out a young calf to rope.

"This is it," she muttered. She swung the rope and tossed ... and missed. "Dang."

"Try again. Go for that little guy over there."

She jerked around. Holt, mounted on an unfamiliar horse, spoke from behind. "You got it," she said. This time her toss dropped square over the calf's head. Petunia immediately backed up, pulling the youngster from the herd.

Frank joined the team on the ground. "Just grab a handful of skin, fore and aft, and flip the calf on his side," he instructed. "One of you take the head and pull his front leg toward it. Someone else, take the hind leg."

Awkwardly they followed Frank's instructions. Once they'd successfully secured the calf, Gabby approached with the branding iron. Another wrangler handled the vaccination and set the bawling critter free. The calf made a beeline for his anxious mother.

"Whatcha waitin' for, Tex?" Holt demanded. "Get your next calf."

This one, larger than the last, proved more difficult to rope, evading every one of Cami's attempts.

"You need to heel him," Holt explained, coming up beside her. "Swing your loop alongside Petunia high and slow. Take your time so you don't rile the herd." He demonstrated, circling his rope level with his shoulder. "Ease it under the calf right in front of his hind legs and jerk hard as soon as his hooves hit the middle of the circle."

Snaring the struggling critter, Holt dragged him over to the ground team. This time Frank stood back and let the guests flip the calf and hold it for branding. Assured they'd gotten the knack of wrassling, he retreated to the top rail of the corral fence to watch.

Cami continued to rope the calves. The smaller ones, which she could catch around the neck gave her little trouble. It was the larger ones she had to heel, that were the problem. Time after time, Holt came up beside her and caught the ones she missed.

Once again he was being proved right. She had no experience. No wonder he refused to think of her as a cowboy. How could he, when she couldn't perform the simplest of cowboy duties?

She progressed through the herd, fighting the dust kicked up by the milling animals. The plaintive bleats of the calves mingled with the concerned moos of their mothers. The stench of burned hide hung thick in the air. The sooner they finished this job, the better she'd like it.

Attempting to heel an escaping calf, she dropped the rope directly in the path of his hind legs. The second he stepped in the loop, she pulled up sharply. To her utter amazement, she caught herself a calf.

"I did it!" she shouted. "I got one!"

From his position on the railing, Frank stood, whooping in delight. Just then a cow slammed against the wooden rail. Frank teetered, fighting for balance. It proved an unsuccessful fight. He fell into the milling cattle, disappearing beneath surging beasts. A cloud of dust concealed him from view.

Standing at the far rail, Charlotte screamed.

CHAPTER NINE

REACTING INSTANTLY, Cami kicked Petunia in the rump and cut through the herd with desperate speed. "You, cow! Get away from him!" she shouted. "Haul your tail outta there. You tromp on anything vital and I'll turn you into hamburger."

"Over here," she heard Frank groan, from somewhere beneath a young steer.

Pulling up alongside, she shooed away the Hereford and offered a hand. Grasping her wrist in an iron grip, Frank swung up behind her, his right arm pressed to his ribs. Carefully she rode to the far side of the corral.

Charlotte ran to the gate and swung it open. She took one look at Frank's bruised and scratched face, and promptly burst into tears.

He slid off Petunia. "Stop your caterwauling, woman," he ordered sternly. "I'll live."

"This time," Charlotte flashed back, through her tears. "What about next time?"

Frank grabbed her by the shoulders and gave her a quick shake. "Gol'durn it, Charlie, I have had it! I'm clear out of patience with you. I've gotten through the past forty-five years and lived to tell the tale. Whether you believe me or not, I aim to get through the next forty-five the same way. If you want to share any of those years, you're going to have to get over your fears.

Because I don't have time to hold your hand and reassure you every time I take a spill.''

To Cami's everlasting astonishment, her sweet, southern, *proper* momma opened her mouth and shouted, ''Who says I want to share anything with you?''

''I do!'' With that Frank tossed her over his uninjured shoulder. Glancing around at the stunned crowd, he inclined his head. ''If you'll excuse us, we have a detail or two to work through in private,'' he said and stomped across the yard toward his horse. A moment later, he and Charlotte were sharing a saddle.

Cami watched them disappear over the ridge. ''Well!'' she exclaimed. ''Well! My goodness. Who would have thought?''

''Get on with you, Tex,'' Gabby groused. ''Those two have been circling each other like a pair of wary dogs ever since your momma first stepped foot on the place. A blind man could have seen it.''

''You talk too much, old man,'' Holt muttered, pulling up beside Cami. He shot her a look of concern. ''You okay?''

''You think she loves him?'' Cami asked in wonder, staring after her mother.

''Let's go for a little ride,'' Holt suggested. He urged his mount into an easy trot and Cami fell in beside him. ''Would it upset you if she did love Frank?''

Cami frowned, considering. ''Not really. I always figured Momma hadn't remarried because she loved my poppa so much no one could replace him. Maybe I was wrong.''

''I wouldn't say you were wrong. Just a bit off base.'' He hesitated, eyeing her keenly. ''She must have been widowed pretty young.''

"Twenty-two."

"And she's never had a serious relationship since?" Cami shook her head and Holt frowned. "That's a long time to be without a man. Think maybe there could be another reason she didn't remarry?"

Cami regarded him with an intent gaze. "You think she was afraid, don't you? That it wasn't only love for Poppa that kept her single, but fear of getting hurt again."

He nodded. "Makes sense doesn't it? Isn't that why she came here? Because she feared you'd be injured in a ranch accident, like your father?"

"Yes," she admitted.

He reined in beneath a widespread cottonwood and leaned across the saddle horn. "Care to hear how I see it?"

"Okay."

"I don't think she hung around the A-OK out of worry for you alone. I think she also stayed because of Frank. I think she fell in love with another cowman and couldn't decide which was worse. Leaving that love behind, or staying and facing her deepest fear—of losing another man to a ranching accident."

"She was afraid to love and lose again." She cleared her throat and said daringly, "Sort of like you."

He reared back and his horse danced beneath him, pawing at the ground. "We were discussin' Charlotte. Let's stick to that, shall we?"

She took his rebuff with good grace. "Right before the Western Roundup dance Momma talked about returning home, but she didn't. I couldn't understand why. I guess this explains it."

"She fell in love with Frank."

"It would seem so." Cami grinned. "She sure didn't stay because of me. She'd already concluded I could take care of myself."

His eyes narrowed. "And just how did she come to that conclusion?"

Cami shrugged. "She knows cowboying is in my blood."

"That tears it!" He crushed his hat low on his head. "Tex, you and me are gonna straighten out this misconception of yours once and for all. Cowboying is in your blood, is that what you believe?"

"With all my heart."

"And I assume cowboying was in your father's blood. And that cowboying is in Frank's blood. But look what happened to them." He waited for that to sink in, then snagged her reins, drawing her close to emphasize his point. His eyes were fixed on hers, his expression stern and relentless. "Ranch life is dangerous even for a skilled cowboy. And, Tex, you aren't even close to skilled. Get too cocky and you put not only yourself in jeopardy, but others as well."

"I'd never, *ever* deliberately hurt someone," Cami insisted, shocked. "Why, whopping that snake just about broke my heart."

"I'm not saying you'd be neglectful on purpose. I am saying that out here ignorance can kill."

They were chilling words, words she was forced to heed. "You know I try my best," she said in a low voice. "And you know that I love this life more than anything."

"I do know you try," he assured her. "And I know that right now you believe this life-style is the best there is. But that's because it's a dream you want to fulfill, a connection between you and your father. But for me, it's a permanent way of life. Once you've played out your fantasy and proven to yourself that you're daddy's little cowboy, you can pack up and leave. I'm here for good.''

She sat rigid in the saddle, defiance in every line of her body. "You're wrong. And one of these days you'll eat those words, mister. Whether you're willing to face it or not, you are like Momma. You're afraid of repeating a past mistake, the same as she is." She nailed him with a cool, direct stare. "But a cowboy, a *real* cowboy, isn't afraid of anything."

And with that, she snatched her reins free and turned Petunia's head toward home.

"AFTERNOON TEA," Agnes muttered, banging a kettle onto the stove. "Since when do we serve afternoon tea? Where the blue blazes does she think she is, anyway?"

Cami sat at the table arranging wafer-thin lemon slices onto a tray. "Momma's just excited."

The housekeeper's expression soured. "About what?"

"It's a surprise."

"Well, I don't like surprises." Agnes switched her aggression to Frank. "And what are you doing here?" She didn't wait for a response. "Takin' up space, that's what you're doin'."

"Yes, ma'am."

"Your ranch is thatta way, in case you've forgotten." She jerked her thumb south.

"Yes, ma'am. Sure is." He yanked on his collar. "That tray ready yet, Tex? Charlie'd like it in the parlor."

"Sure thing." She handed it over.

Agnes whipped around. "Parlor? What parlor's that? We don't have a parlor!" she shouted at Frank's rapidly retreating back. She stomped to the sink, muttering beneath her breath. "Flowers takin' up every one of my good pitchers. Next she'll have candles dripping all over my table. Well, I won't stand for it, you hear?"

"They can hear you in Alaska," Holt said, striding into the kitchen. "What's all the hollerin' about?"

"Hollerin'?" The housekeeper advanced in his direction. "You haven't begun to hear hollerin'. You know what that silly twitter bug of a woman wants? I'll tell you what she wants. She wants four-petties. What in tarnation's a pettie, I'd like to know?"

"It's a—"

"Never you mind." She waved a soup spoon in the air. "It don't matter what it is. I'm not fixing it. Fact is, I'm not fixing another blamed thing until that banty hen's back scratchin' in her own yard."

"You'd let the guests starve?" Holt demanded.

"Darned tootin' I would! I'm going to my sister's place. When Miss Fancy Pants decides to hightail her citified caboose outta my path, I'll consider returning. In the meantime, you can go whistle for your vittles." With that she slammed down the spoon and snatched off her apron.

Cami sighed. She'd learned from their occasional run-ins that Agnes was more bluff than action. The crusty housekeeper just needed to feel needed, to feel one of the family. "They're going to announce their engagement," she explained.

Agnes stopped dead. "Come again?"

"Momma and Frank. That's the surprise. That's why she'd like everything all elegant and everything. They're going to announce their engagement."

"Well...well..." Temporarily speechless, Agnes sat down at the table. "You don't say. Why doesn't anybody tell me these things? Don't I count any more?" She rounded on Holt. "Did you know about this?"

He shrugged. "I suspected."

She shook her head in wonder. "I'll be. A weddin'." She sniffed, dabbing the corner of her eye with a dishrag. "I always did have a soft spot for a weddin'."

"Momma's being very brave," Cami said, shooting a sidelong glance at Holt. "Ever since Poppa died, she's been a bit gun-shy."

Agnes nodded sagely. "She's not the only one. I know someone else who's gun-shy when it comes to trippin' down the aisle again."

"It's because of that city slicker," Cami said.

"They're the ruination of many a fine man," the housekeeper concurred, with a surprisingly companionable nod. "A rancher needs a proper wife who'll stick by him through the hard times as well as the good." She stared at Cami, her eyes narrowing. "Somebody like you, Tex."

So she'd finally been accepted by the ornery woman. Cami buried a smile. "You're forgetting. I'm a city slicker, too."

"Maybe. But you're a cowboy at heart," Agnes insisted, giving her official stamp of approval.

"That's not possible," Cami heaved a sigh. "I have it on very good authority that cowboys are heartless."

Agnes reared back. "Who told you that?" she exclaimed.

"Holt."

He hurled his hat to the floor. "That's not what I said and you damned well know it!"

Cami jumped to her feet. "You said that cowboying isn't in the blood or in the heart. But if it's not there, I'd like to know just where the heck it is."

He thrust his face into hers. "I said, you crazy female, that cowboying is a learned skill, not a state of mind."

"You think a body can't be a cowboy unless they're born and grow up on a ranch." She planted her hands on her hips, refusing to back down. "Well, I'm here to tell you, you're wrong!"

Agnes looked from one to the other. Then she folded her arms across her ample bosom. "Amen to that, sister," she said, with a decisive switch of allegiance.

He spun in his tracks. "You have a hell of a lot to say, for somebody who doesn't work for me any more." Then he turned on Cami, jabbing an index finger beneath her nose. "As for you... I won't be conned by another city slicker. You may fool Agnes with your cowboy act, but you don't fool me."

"Huh!" Agnes snorted. "The only fool I see is standing there flappin' his jaw."

Holt picked up his Stetson and slapped it on his head. "Woman, if you hadn't already quit, you'd be fired." And with that, he strode from the room.

"Don't threaten me!" Agnes shot after him. "Or I'll really quit. And then where'd you be? Up a creek, that's where." With a satisfied smile at having gotten the final word, she tied her apron around her ample waist and returned to the stove. "Now. What the Sam Hill's a pettie, do you suppose? Pull my cookbook off that shelf over there, Tex, and look it up. We've an engagement party to plan."

A WEEK PASSED AND NOTHING changed. Though Cami continued to revel in ranch life, she longed to share her excitement and enthusiasm with Holt. But he'd erected a barrier between them, a barrier she couldn't seem to circumvent.

Slowly determination built. Somehow, someway she'd prove him wrong, prove that she belonged on a ranch, that this life-style was as much a part of her, as it was a part of him. So she bided her time and quietly went about her job, perfecting her skills, always intent on finding a way to win him over.

The morning of the weekly wiener roast she noticed him exiting the ranch house wearing a business suit. She pulled up short, her mouth falling open.

"Good golly," she breathed. "That you, Holt?"

"It's me, all right." His dark eyes gleamed with amusement. "Close your mouth, Tex. The flies around here are none too tasty."

"You're in a business suit."

"Now, don't rub it in," he carped good-naturedly. "Sheer necessity is the only reason I'd torture myself wearing these city duds."

She circled him. Six feet and three inches of raw, lean muscle filled out a business suit real fine, she decided. Black pinstripe strained across his broad shoulders and molded the powerful muscles of his thighs. A thick leather belt with a rodeo buckle encircled his lean hips. And at his throat, a large silver-rimmed piece of onyx anchored the braided bola that substituted for a necktie. The only familiar articles he wore were his black Stetson and his boots.

"You sure do look swell," she said in admiration. "Going someplace special?"

"Not to my way of thinking. I have a business meeting with some cattle brokers. I've found it's smart to look the part of the prosperous cowman. For some reason, they give me a better price."

She frowned. "But what about this afternoon's horseback ride and wiener roast? Will you return in time for that?"

"I'll have to give it a miss, I'm afraid. Gabby can lead it."

Cami clasped her hands together, a sudden thought occurring to her. It was perfect. The perfect way to impress Holt with her improved cowboy skills. "Would you let me lead it, instead?" she asked, trying not to sound too much like she was begging. Even if she was.

He didn't hesitate for a second. "No."

She talked fast. "I remember where to take them. I've been there at least a half-dozen times. You just go over the ridge to the rock with the moss mustache and hang a left. Go down the gully past that funny stump that looks like a porcupine with his quills in an uproar. Turn right. Sing one verse of 'The Worms Crawl In.' Hang a sharp left and we're there. Am I right?"

"Right. No."

She talked faster. "Once there, I have everyone dismount. Build a fire—you taught me how yourself, if you remember. Roast the wieners. I hardly burn 'em at all any more and I'd be extra careful this time. That should count for something, don't you think? And I have the songs we're supposed to sing down pat. Eat. I handle the eating part real well. Put out the fire. Come home. What's so hard about that?"

"Nothing," he said flatly. "But you'd find a way to screw it up, anyway."

It was difficult to argue with fact. "Aw, Holt..."

He shook his head. "You're not experienced enough. Gabby will lead the group."

Crestfallen, she nodded. "Yessir, boss. Whatever you say."

He smiled encouragingly. "You're doing fine, Tex. No need to rush it. There's plenty of time."

"Is there?" she whispered forlornly. "The summer's half gone already."

"Which leaves us half a summer to go. I'm going to miss my appointment. We can discuss this again later."

She watched him walk away and straightened her shoulders, setting her mouth in a firm line. Oh, they'd discuss it later, all right. She'd see to it. Because one of these days, she'd prove herself capable. One of these days, she'd impress the heck out of him.

TWO HOURS LATER, Gabby and the adults were saddled and ready to leave. The only holdup was the children who hadn't returned from their hayride.

"If we're going to have the wiener roast and get back before dark, we'll have to push off soon," Gabby complained. "Who's pulling that hay wagon, anyway? Josh? He knows better than to run late."

"Look," Cami said, pointing down the dirt road. "I see their dust. Why don't I saddle the children's horses and you all go ahead. We'll follow right behind."

Gabby scratched his jaw. "I'm not so sure that's a good idea, Tex. No point in taking unnecessary chances. We can wait for them. There should be enough time."

"But if you leave now," Cami argued, "you can get the fire started and we won't be so rushed. If you wait for the children, we'll have to tear out there, hurry and eat and tear back. How much fun is that?"

He frowned. "I don't know what Holt would say about splittin' the group," he muttered. "I surely don't."

She offered her most confident and winning smile. "I can handle this. I'm positive. Besides, we'll catch up with you in no time." Which might help square things with Holt when he heard about this, she thought, suppressing a guilty twinge.

More importantly, it would be the perfect opportunity to prove how good a cowboy she was once and for all. Holt would be impressed. He'd be proud. Maybe he'd even come to love her.

She could dream, couldn't she?

"Well...I guess it'd be okay," Gabby relented.

"Thanks!" Cami exclaimed, and threw her arms around the cowhand.

He thrust her away. "Hey, hey! Whatcha doin'?"

"Hugging you," she replied, bewildered. "Why?"

"Cowboys don't hug," he blustered. "Fact is, cowboys don't even touch. Now keep yer distance." He stomped over to his horse. "Danged female. You have the supplies?"

"In my saddlebags," she assured him. "Wieners, beans, cocoa and marshmallows."

"And I've got the matches." He mounted up. "You'll be right behind?"

"Practically on your tail."

He nodded. "Let's go folks."

Cami hurried into the barn and saddled four horses for the children. Just as she'd finished, the wagon jerked to a stop and three boys and a girl tumbled off the hay and ran to her side.

"Is it time for the wiener roast?"

"Can you show us some more yo-yo tricks?"

"Yes, it's time for the wiener roast. And, no, no tricks until we catch up with your parents. They've gone ahead. So, run inside and get a drink. Use the facilities if you have to, but move along."

Fifteen minutes later they were ready to leave. Cami made sure they had sweaters and sunscreen, that they'd filled their canteens and wore their hats. Satisfied that everyone was in fine fettle, she led the way into the mountains.

"Okay, kids, over the ridge to the rock with the moss mustache."

"Hey, Tex," Nathan called. "You bring extra yo-yos with you?"

"Does a horse swat flies with his tail?" she scoffed. "Of course I brought extra yo-yos. Why, by the time I'm done with you four, you'll amaze and delight your friends back home. I'll bet—"

"Is that the rock with the mustache?" asked Katie Sue, pointing.

Cami stared. "By golly, so it is. Hang a right everybody and head down into that gully. When you see a big, old stump that looks like a pincushion, give a holler. Now where was I? Oh, yeah. You'll amaze and delight your friends back home. Why, I'll bet—"

"There's the stump!" Aaron cried.

Cami stopped and studied it. It seemed smaller. But how many stumps could there be with a bejillion branches sticking out of it? Maybe the lack of rain over the past week had caused it to shrink a bit. "Terrific job, Aaron. Turn left. Now for the important part. Everybody has to sing a rousing chorus of 'The Worms Crawl In.' It's the only way I can tell how far before our last turn."

The children sang with gusto. "One more time!" Gary shouted.

Cami frowned. One more time? They should be at the final turn by now. Yet it was nowhere in sight. "I think we've gone too far," she said. "I'll tell you what. Let's go back the way we came. We can repeat the song and when we're done, we'll be at the porcupine stump again."

"The one like a pincushion?" Katie Sue asked.

"Yep. So keep an eye out for it, okay?"

They wended their way through that song, another about *eating* worms, and a third that involved rearranging various body parts in strange and uncomfortable positions.

They never did find the stump.

Cami tried her best to hide her concern, not wanting to frighten the children. But as it grew later and later and the sun slid relentlessly behind the mountains, she became seriously alarmed. Soon it was a struggle to pick their way across the rock-strewn terrain.

"I'm hungry," Nathan spoke up.

"Me, too," the others agreed.

"Aren't we there yet?" Katie Sue, the youngest, looked distinctly tearful.

Cami reined in Petunia. "No, I'm afraid we're not." She studied the surrounding landscape and came to a fast decision. "I've got an idea," she announced. "Let's have an adventure."

The boys glanced at each other, excited. Katie Sue didn't appear quite as thrilled. "What kind of adventure?" Aaron asked.

"A camping-out kind of adventure. See that nice open spot over the next ridge?" She pointed to a level area at the top of a grassy knoll. "We'll park our horses there and build a roaring fire and eat our wieners and beans. After that we'll toast marshmallows and drink cocoa and sing more songs."

"All right!" Gary exclaimed. "Food."

"I'll sing," Katie Sue consented. "But no more worm songs."

"Fair enough. No more worm songs." Cami led the way to their chosen camping spot and dismounted. "Before we do anything else, there's something that comes first. Who knows what it is?"

Nathan scratched his nose. "Firewood."

"Phone Mommy and tell her what time I'll be home."

"The wieners."

Aaron gave it great thought. "Take care of the horses," he finally said.

Cami grinned. "You got it, buster. Horses first, firewood second, wieners last."

"What about phoning Mommy?" Katie Sue wanted to know.

"That might be a little more difficult." She decided to stall. "We'll discuss it over dinner."

After watering the horses at a nearby stream, stripping them of their saddles and allowing them to graze, Cami had the children collect a plentiful supply of firewood.

"What about matches?" Aaron asked.

For an instant, Cami panicked. Gabby had the matches. And without matches there'd be no fire. No fire. No food. No warmth. And no light to comfort the children through the long night. She fought for control. *Take it easy! Think. What did they do before matches?* Maybe she could rub two sticks together.

She folded her arms across her chest and shook her head pityingly. "You city slickers are all alike. You have to use a match to build a simple fire. That's truly pathetic."

Gary lifted his chin. "Says who? I'm a Boy Scout. We always come prepared." With that, he stuck a hand in his pocket and pulled out a flint. "Just watch."

He gathered a large supply of dry leaves and tiny twigs and arranged them in a loose mound. Aaron and Nathan quickly followed his example. So did Katie Sue, though with a bit more reluctance.

To Cami's amazement, Gary soon had a tiny flame flickering to life at the base of the mound. He fed the flame with more leaves and twigs and before long had a small fire going. It didn't take much to build it from a small fire to a large roaring one.

"If that don't beat all," she muttered. Working quickly, she formed a good-size fire ring with stones. "Get sticks for the wieners. I'll open the cans of beans and warm them up. We'll be chowing down before you know it."

Dark had just settled in when they finished off the last hot dog and scooped up the last bean. Nathan and Gary started on the marshmallows. Katie Sue stole close to Cami for a cuddle.

"Okay, kids, time to talk," Cami announced.

Aaron gazed at her from across the fire. "We're lost, aren't we?" he asked.

Katie Sue started in alarm. "I wouldn't call it lost, exactly," Cami hastened to correct, reassuring the little girl with a hug. "Let's just say we're temporarily mislaid."

"What does that mean?" Nathan questioned.

"It means," she confessed, "that tomorrow Holt will come and help us find our way back to the ranch. Until then, we get to stay up late and tell stories and sleep under the stars. How does that sound?"

"Decent!" Gary said.

Greatly encouraged, she expanded on the idea. "We'll use our saddles for pillows and sleep on our saddle blankets, like real cowboys."

"What if I get cold?" Katie Sue demanded fretfully.

"It's going to be pretty warm tonight, but we've got the fire in case it turns chilly. And you can always snuggle close to me." To Cami's relief, the little girl relaxed. "Okay, boys, look through the saddlebags and find my yo-yos. There's one for each of you. Who wants to learn 'dunk the doughnut'?"

"I would! I would!" Nathan shouted.

"Forget 'dunk the doughnut,' Tex," a deep voice spoke from the darkness. At the same time Git burst through the circle of children, barking hysterically.

Cami shot to her feet. "Holt?" she gasped. "Is that you?"

He stepped into the firelight, the leaping flames casting a devilish glow across his hard, furious features. "Oh, yeah, Tex. It's me. And instead of 'dunk the doughnut,' why don't you show them 'hang the wrangler.' Better yet, why don't *I* show them."

CHAPTER TEN

CAMI CLEARED HER THROAT. "I don't believe I know that one. Fact is, I don't believe I *want* to know that one." As an afterthought, she buried her yo-yo deep in her pocket.

Holt glanced around. "You kids all right?"

"We're having an adventure," Gary announced.

"I want my mommy," Katie Sue said, and promptly burst into tears.

Cami rushed to comfort the child, but Holt beat her to it. He scooped the youngster into his arms and brushed her hair from her damp face. "Easy does it, buckaroo. Everything's going to be all right now. I promise."

The tears slowed. "Can we go home?"

"In the morning. It's not a good idea to travel at night. Would you like to tell your folks you're safe? It would be a little like talking to them." She nodded, and he carried her to his horse. Opening a saddlebag, he pulled out a flare gun.

"We're going to talk to Mommy with a gun?" Katie Sue asked dubiously.

"Sure are. You watch." They crossed to a clearing and he aimed into the air. "Say when, and I'll pull the trigger. It'll make a loud boom and set the sky ablaze, like fireworks. Everyone at the ranch will see it and re-alize I've found you and you're all fine."

She covered her ears with her hands. "Okay. Shoot it."

He did. Instantly a bright flash shot skyward. All eyes were riveted on the glowing red ball that burst across the night canopy. Just as the final twinkling ember drifted to earth, an answering flare streaked high overhead.

"See," he said, pointing. "There's your mother's answer. She knows you're safe and is saying goodnight."

Katie Sue sighed and snuggled against his shoulder. "G'night, Mommy."

Cami gazed at the ground, tears stinging her eyes. This was her fault. She'd done this. She'd never felt more ashamed in her life. All those worried parents. All that fear and anxiety. All because of her.

"Have you eaten?" he asked the group at large.

"We ate wieners and beans and marshmallows and hot chocolate." Aaron catalogued. "I'm stuffed."

"We've been having lots of fun," Nathan added earnestly. "Tex was going to show us some yo-yo tricks before we went to bed. Wanna watch?"

"Sounds good. Let me get Loco settled and I'll join you." He looked directly at Cami and she flinched beneath his hard gaze. "I have bedrolls for the kids. Come and get them."

She gulped. Why hadn't he just said, "Come and get them and die?" Dragging behind, she left the protective circle of firelight and was instantly swallowed by the menacing darkness. She shivered, not from the chill of the night air but from the cold eyes and tense stance of the man in front of her.

"Holt—"

"Don't say a word." He kept his voice low, but his warning cracked like a whip. "First answer this. Is everyone safe?"

"Yes."

"Uninjured?"

"Yes."

"Not even a scratch?"

"Not even a scratch," she was quick to reassure.

He grabbed a fistful of shirt, tugging her close. "You scared the hell out of me, woman. You know that?"

"I'm sorry, I—"

"Shut up, Tex."

Without another word, he wrapped his arms around her and kissed her with a desperation she couldn't mistake. She forgot everything except how good it felt to be held by him, loved by him, to be with the one man who made her whole, made her complete. She loved this man. Lordy, how she loved him.

Minutes passed. Finally, she rested her forehead against his chest, listening to the rapid, powerful beat of his heart. "I'm sorry about what happened," she said. "I'd like to explain."

Instantly his muscles tautened and he thrust her away. "Don't."

"Holt?" she whispered, bewildered by the abrupt change in him.

"I'm warning you. Let it drop."

"But, I thought..."

He rounded on her. "You thought what? That that kiss lets you off the hook? Think again." The harshness in his tone made her cringe. "Now listen up, and listen good. You aren't to offer one word of excuse about this...this *adventure* in front of the children. You keep it light and friendly. Tomorrow—" he leaned closer "—tomorrow we *will* discuss it. Long and hard."

"Yessir, boss," she murmured. "Long and hard." He tossed the bedrolls at her and she clutched them to her chest. Tears clogged her throat and burned her eyes. She forced herself to speak, shocked at how ragged her voice sounded. "For what it's worth, I've learned my lesson."

"No, I don't think you have," he replied coolly, stripping the saddle off Loco. "But come morning, you will."

She stumbled back into camp and gave each child a bedroll, helping them arrange their sleeping spots. Then she passed out the yo-yos and quietly set about teaching them some of her simpler tricks. Eventually Holt joined in. But it wasn't long before Katie Sue, battling yawns, sought her bed. The three boys weren't far behind.

Holt shifted closer to the fire, banking it for the night. Cami settled onto her saddle blanket and watched. A breeze caught at the upper reaches of the trees, rustling the leaves. In the distance a great horned owl hooted. The fire snapped and sparks leapt into the air. Holt lifted his head, his gaze meeting hers.

"I know you don't want to hear this, but I'm sorry," she said softly. "Truly sorry."

He shoved back his hat and nodded. "I know you are, Tex. But you disobeyed my direct order just to prove a point about your worth as a cowboy. Well, you did that, all right." He tossed a stick at the fire. "But the sad fact is, you proved just the opposite of what you'd hoped. And you put these kids in jeopardy to do it."

She didn't say another word. Instead she hunkered down on top of the blanket, battling guilt and grief. Honesty compelled her to admit the truth. She *had* been trying to prove a point, one aimed directly at Holt. And she *had* used the children in order to do it. And in so doing, she *had* put them at risk.

She wasn't worthy of being a cowboy.

"Good night, Holt," she whispered.

"Night, Tex." He hesitated, then added gently, "Sweet dreams."

She squeezed her eyes shut. Not likely. Seemed she was plumb out of dreams, sweet or otherwise.

A WAKE-UP LICK FROM Git rousted Cami at the crack of dawn. She busied herself heating water in the rinsed bean cans and preparing hot chocolate and trail mix for breakfast. Then she watered and saddled the horses. The children took more effort. Still, she managed to deal with their morning grumpies and get them fed, spit polished and ready to go, hoping her hard work would help atone for her poor judgment.

Holt crossed to her side and handed her a tin cup. "I know you don't drink coffee. Thought you might like to make an exception this morning. It's instant."

"Thanks," she said gruffly and took a quick swallow. It tasted even worse than she remembered, but she forced herself to drink it. Before this day ended, she'd need the caffeine.

"Roll up your beds," Holt told the children, "and douse the fire with dirt. Gary, you make sure it's done right." He turned cool, stern eyes in Cami's direction. "Tex and I are going for a quick stroll. You kids don't budge from this spot. Understand?"

As one, the children nodded solemnly. Cami could tell from their expressions that they'd obey his order to the letter. He snagged her arm and led the way out of camp.

"Where are we going?" she asked anxiously.

"You'll know when we get there." They walked about a hundred feet. "What do you see?"

She stopped and glanced around, bewildered. "Woods to both sides. A clearing up ahead."

"Take another look at that clearing." He tugged her a step closer.

Cami gasped, scrambling back. A yard in front of her the ground abruptly ended, plunging to a very deep, narrow and practically invisible chasm. "Oh, Lordy," she gulped.

"Which way were you traveling yesterday?"

She paled. "This way."

"I thought as much," he said with a nod. "You wouldn't have seen the drop coming until it opened beneath you. You realize that, don't you?"

She couldn't speak. Instead, she clapped a hand over her mouth and nodded, fighting a sharp, near overwhelming bout of nausea.

"If for some reason you'd chosen to detour into the woods, you'd have hit this same gorge there, too," he continued relentlessly. "The accident would've been avoidable, because the drop's more visible. Not that that matters. Because unless you'd decided to go back the way you came, eventually you would have returned here, on the only path that looks navigable. Then you and the children would have ridden for a fall."

She fought for breath. "I didn't know. I'm sorry," she gasped.

"I believe you, Tex. But let me make one more point. What we're doing here," he swept his arm to encompass the surrounding territory, "isn't even true cowboy work. This is taking folks for a pleasant ride in the mountains. Cowboy work is much more. It involves dangerous animals and machinery and adverse weather conditions. It requires skill and care, and most important of all, thought."

Cami bowed her head. "I admit to a lack in one or two of those areas."

He muttered an unflattering comment. "The fact is, you're lacking in all those areas. Period. You don't think, Tex. And cowboys who don't think, don't live long enough to regret it. A wrangler has to be able to count on his fellow wranglers, has to trust them with his very life at times. I can't have someone I don't trust workin' for me. It's as simple as that."

"Holt, please ..."

He didn't relent. "Your time for explanations is over. You stand here while I finish getting us packed. And you think about what I've said. We leave in five minutes." With that, he turned and stalked away.

Cami stared at the yawning pit in front of her. She and the children could have been down there, hurt and broken...or worse. And it would have been all her fault, because she'd been so bent on proving her worth. Well, she'd done that, hadn't she?

Holt was right. She didn't deserve to be a cowboy. Who was she kidding? She *wasn't* a cowboy. Which left her with one option and only one option. She stiffened her spine. First things first. Time to face her mistakes.

She whistled for Git and returned to camp, inspecting the site for anything they might have left behind. She checked to be sure the fire was properly extinguished and all evidence of their passing erased. A bit of plastic lay on the ground and she picked it up, shoving it in her pocket.

"Shake a leg," Holt called. "We've several hours of riding to go."

By midmorning, they arrived at the ranch—a happy, chattering group, all except for a silent, abashed Cami. Approaching the first of the cabins Holt drew to a stop.

"You kids go ahead and let your folks know you're safe." He waited until they'd ridden off before addressing Cami. "If you'd rather, you can cut around the back way."

For an instant, she didn't understand what he meant. Then hot color flooded her face. "I'm no coward," she stated fiercely. "I made a mistake and I'll own up to it." She kicked Petunia in the rump and trotted after the children, rejoining them just as they reached the barn.

The parents came running from the ranch house, gathering around the children. Two of the mothers were crying. The fathers' faces were set in identical relieved yet weary lines. She doubted a single one had gotten any sleep. Remorse consumed her.

"Excuse me, folks," she spoke in a loud, clear voice. They turned and looked at her, their expressions ranging from anger to suspicion.

"Are you the girl who got our kids lost?" Katie Sue's mother demanded.

Holt reined in beside her, but she pointedly ignored him. "I am. And I'd like to offer my most sincere apologies. I'd also like to assure you that Mr. Winston had no idea I'd taken on such a huge responsibility. And he'd never have approved, if he had known. I hope you won't hold him accountable since it was entirely my own doing. I have no excuse...." She shrugged. "Leastwise none that would make anyone any happier about this whole unfortunate situation. But I do regret my actions. I'm sorry."

"Don't be mad, Mommy," Katie Sue said, tugging at the woman's arm. "We had fun. I want to do it again."

The unexpected statement brought quick laughter and helped ease some of the tension. Holt took advantage of the temporary lull. "If anyone has any questions or concerns, you address them to me." He glanced at Cami and murmured. "Go take care of the horses, Tex. The sooner you're out of sight, the sooner this will blow over."

Obediently Cami led the animals into the barn and set to work. No need to hurry. Only one other job remained—to talk to her mother. And that could wait a little longer. An hour later, she crossed to the ranch house. She expected to find Charlotte in an absolute panic and weeping buckets. Instead Cami found her mother calmly discussing wedding cakes with Agnes.

"Momma, may I speak to you for a minute?"

"Back from your little escapade, are you?" Agnes said, slapping closed her cookbook. "Half the town's been callin' for updates. I told 'em you were probably dead at the bottom of some gulch and good riddance."

"Thank you."

The housekeeper snorted. "They didn't believe me, neither. They're on their way, you know. I think they're hopin' to see a lynchin'."

"They probably will."

Agnes's eyes narrowed and she planted her hands on her hips. "You realize what their comin' means, don't you? It means I'll have to brew up gallons of coffee. Everyone was up so late worryin' about you, they're plumb tuckered out this morning."

"You could just shoot me and save everyone a lot of misery," Cami suggested.

"Well...well..." the housekeeper sputtered, and turned to Charlotte. "Call the doc, Charlie. The girl's sick as a gut-swollen mule."

"I don't need a doctor. I need to talk." She managed a smile. "Momma, could we?"

Her mother stood and linked arms. "Why don't we go to my room?" she suggested. "I'll return shortly, Agnes. But I really would appreciate it if you'd consider the strawberry whipped icing."

"I'll consider it," Agnes said pleasantly enough, before muttering beneath her breath, "when hell freezes over."

"You had everyone very upset," Charlotte remarked, stepping into her bedroom and closing the door behind them.

"Yes, Momma, I know. I'm sorry about that." She should just stamp the words on her forehead and be done with it.

"I knew, of course, that you'd be perfectly safe," her mother continued, clearly pleased with herself. "After all, cowboying is in your blood, as you've reminded me so many times."

Cami groaned to hear her own words parroted back. She climbed onto the bed, hugging her knees to her chest. "I've changed my mind about that. I'm afraid the Greenbush cowboying gene must have skipped a generation or something." She looked up at Charlotte, tears filling her eyes. "Oh, Momma, I've been such a fool. I've hurt Holt and I've jeopardized those poor kids and upset their parents and gotten the whole town in a tizzy. And for what?"

"So you could prove to Holt you're a cowboy and worth hanging on to."

"So that I could..." She stared at her mother. "You know?"

"I think most of Lullabye has it figured out by now."

Cami nodded. "Naturally."

Charlotte sat down and put an arm around her daughter, giving her a tender hug. "Oh, sweetie, it's not that bad. Has Holt fired you?"

"Not in so many words. But he was so mad he had trouble even speaking." She dropped her chin to her knees. "Give him time."

"Trust me. If Holt Winston hasn't found the words yet, he's never going to. You made a little mistake. He'll forgive you and everything will be back to normal."

Cami shook her head. "You don't understand. All these years, I've been kidding myself. But I'm finally facing reality. I'm no cowboy. I never was. Hell's bells. After this latest fiasco, I don't even deserve to be Texan."

Charlotte stiffened. "Oh, dear," she murmured faintly.

Cami frowned. "You've gone all white and funny looking. What's wrong?"

Her mother's arm slid away and she twisted her diamond engagement ring. "It...it seemed harmless enough at the time."

"What seemed harmless enough at the time?" Cami asked, bewildered.

"I...I mean, your daddy was a Texan and if we hadn't been visiting my mother at the time, and if I hadn't gotten my dates mixed up... It seemed so important to you, that I didn't have the heart to tell you..."

A horrible, impossible, distressing suspicion took hold. Cami swallowed. "Tell me what, Momma?"

"You aren't precisely a Texan. Legally, I mean," Charlotte confessed. "You were born in Richmond. But... but that's okay, isn't it? I mean your father was a Texan, so that has to count, doesn't it? It makes you a sort of Texan, right? A... a step-Texan or half Texan or something?"

"Not... not..." She couldn't take it in.

"Camellia? Sweetheart?" Her mother's voice rose. "Cami? Are you okay?"

"I think I'm going to be sick."

It felt like the bottom had fallen out of her world. All this time... All this time she'd thought of herself as a cowboy and as a Texan. She'd thought ranching was in her blood. She'd been so certain that with a little practice her natural-born skills would come to the fore. Now she understood why they never had. What a fool she'd been. And how right Holt had been.

It took all her willpower to stand. "I have to leave now."

Her mother jumped up, wringing her hands. "What precisely do you mean by leave? Go to your room? Is that what you mean?"

"Yep. I'm going to my room now. The one in Richmond." She squared her shoulders. "I'm here under false pretenses. And I'm honor bound to correct that. I'll pack my bags and leave. It'll save everyone a lot of trouble."

"Now, Camellia, there's no sense in doing anything rash."

Cami shook her head, blinking back tears. "Don't you see, Momma? Ever since I was a little girl I thought I was a cowboy. When somebody asked me my name,

I'd tell them I was Cami from Texas, a natural-born cowboy.''

"You can still be that!"

"No. I can't. Because none of it's true. I'm not a cowboy. I'm not even ..." Her chin wobbled. "I'm not even Texan. I'm not quite sure what I am, but I strongly suspect I'm some sort of flowering shrub." She wiped her cheeks, surprised to find her hands damp with tears. "That's going to take a bit of gettin' used to. Maybe when I introduce myself I can say, 'Hi, I'm Camellia Greenbush. Just plant me anywhere.' So long as it isn't near cows or ropes or horses or anything dangerous." Or anyone she loved. She seemed to have an uncanny knack for hurting them, too.

"Sweetheart ..."

"It's okay, Momma." Cami gave her mother a swift hug. "I'll get over it." She forced out a watery laugh. "It's not like I wasn't warned. Holt's been trying to set me straight ever since I got here."

"Don't leave."

Cami bowed her head. "I have to," she whispered. "I can't live a lie. And I can't put Holt and the A-OK at risk. Because that's just what I'd be doing." She looked up, saying resolutely, "But I'm glad you found Frank and put your fears to rest. He's a good man and I know you'll be happy living on a ranch again. I'll be back for the wedding. I promise."

There wasn't anything left to be said. Cami gave her mother a final hug, and then before she could change her mind ran from the room.

"WELL, HOLT," Wes said with a laugh. "You've been a mite busy lately, haven't you?"

"And then some," Holt acknowledged with a grin.

"Cami sure keeps things jumpin'. Ain't that so, Lem?"

"Aw, Tex is the sweetest gal in the world. Look at how she pitched in to set my store to rights. You know what it is? It's that smile of hers. Friendly, open, kind."

"Naw," Gabby said, yanking on his mustache and scowling. "It's those dang dimples. The way they wink at you is enough to drive a man loco."

"Or those eyes. Bluest I've ever seen."

Frank grinned. "And what about those bitty freckles? Ever tried to count 'em?"

"Never you mind those bitty freckles," Holt interrupted. After all, a man could only allow his friends so much liberty.

Reverend Sam folded his arms across his chest. "I suggest you rope that filly to you good and proper before some varmint gets the notion to steal her away."

Hoots of laughter greeted his remark.

"Laugh all you want," Charlotte interrupted, elbowing her way into the group. "But no one's going to get the chance to steal her, because she's left. Hitched a ride to town with Katie Sue's momma."

Holt stuck his thumbs in his belt and rocked back on his heels. "Did she now?"

"Thirty minutes ago," Charlotte confirmed. "She's leaving. For good. Packed her bags and everything. See?" She pointed to Git sitting beside the corral fence, a rope in his mouth. He whined pitifully. "She gave that dog her rope and told me to give you this."

A befeathered pink cowboy hat hung from her fingertips.

Holt froze.

Suddenly he saw before him a choice, a choice as clear and as different as wrong from right. He could continue as before, he realized, protecting his ranch, his way of life and his heart. In his mind's eye he could see it happen, see the uniformed days lined up, stretching before him with a comforting sameness. Along this path, the familiar rhythm of his life would resume, like the rhythm of spring into summer and autumn into winter. And he'd be alone.

Or there was Cami. And along that path lay hope and laughter and joy, and a love so strong it nearly stole his breath. There was only one catch. Treading that path meant trusting a city slicker... trusting her with his ranch, but most risky of all, trusting her with his heart.

And in that moment, he realized there was only one path to choose.

"Thirty minutes ago, you say?" he demanded.

Charlotte nodded. "She plans to catch the noon train."

"The noon train!" Wes exclaimed. "It's eleven-thirty now. You'll never catch her in time."

"We'll see about that." He snatched Cami's hat from Charlotte and ran for his horse. Grabbing Loco's reins, he leapt aboard.

"You're wasting your time," Frank called. "No one's ever made that ride in under thirty-five minutes."

Holt leveled a gimlet-eyed stare at his friend and crushed his hat low on his forehead. "Watch me!"

With that he wheeled Loco around, slammed his heels in the horse's flanks and shot down the drive toward town. Cutting across the pasture he vaulted the gate, never once breaking stride and disappeared over the ridge in a cloud of dust.

CAMI SAT SLUMPED in her seat, feeling decidedly naked without her hat. The train whistle blew, a long, forlorn sound. She heard the last call for boarding and closed her eyes, battling tears. This was it. The death of her dreams.

Just then the door at the end of the train car crashed open. "You can't come in here!" she heard the conductor shout. "You need a ticket. I'll summon the police if you don't get off."

Cami stiffened. It couldn't be. She opened an eye, risking a peek. And there he was.

Holt strode down the aisle, swatting the conductor aside with no more effort than he would a pesky fly. He stopped by her seat. "Ma'am," he said, tipping his hat. "This your luggage?" He pointed to the suitcase on the floor.

She straightened. "Yes. But what are you—" He grabbed her bag in one hand, her wrist in the other and yanked. "Holt! Stop! You can't do this!" She stared up at him uncertainly. "What precisely are you doing?"

"Taking you off this train."

She nodded. "Just checking." Then, "Holt, I can't go back. I've made a mess of everything."

"True." He started down the aisle, dragging her behind.

"I'm no cowboy. I never was."

"Also true."

"Stop a minute, will you? I keep making mistakes."

"Yep. And this was your biggest."

She dug in her heels. "I'm just a city slicker who'll ruin your business if I stay."

That stopped him. He spun in his tracks and dropped her suitcase to the floor. "Now there you're wrong. You might be the sorriest cowboy I ever did see, and you might be the tryingest woman I ever met. But you're also the sweetest and warmest and kindest. My guests love you. My employees love you. Hell, the whole town loves you."

She stared up at him in wonder. "Really?"

"Really." He cleared his throat, his voice gruff. "Besides, you can't leave. You've got a contract to honor. And real cowboys always honor their commitments."

"But I'm not a real cowboy. You said so yourself." She suddenly remembered and tears filled her eyes. "Oh, Holt. I'm not even Texan!"

"Not Texan?" He frowned. "Since when? Who says?"

"Since this morning." She hung her head in shame. "Momma says I was really born in Richmond."

"Well, shoot." He kicked at her suitcase. "Aw, turn off the waterworks, Tex...Cami. Now that you live in Colorado, consider yourself a...a..."

She peeked up. "Colorado-er?"

He shrugged, nonplussed. "Beats me. I guess that's as good a name as any." He turned to the spectators watching with fascination from their seats. "Folks, I'd like you to meet Colorado Cami, an honest-to-goodness cowboy."

"Nice to meet you, Colorado. A pleasure, Cami," voices called.

Holt nodded in satisfaction. "Now it's official, C.C. Can we go?"

"C.C.?"

"Colorado Cami, of course."

She tried to control the hope blossoming to life. "You really want me back?"

"I can't force you," he replied. "But if you're that intent on leaving, you'd best take this." He swept off his hat and dropped it into her hands.

She stared at him in shock. "But...but a cowboy *never* gives up his hat."

Holt inclined his head. "Leastwise, not unless he's too dead to fight for it."

"I...I don't understand."

"Keep it." He stared down at her and the warm, passionate expression in his black eyes stole her breath clean away. A fire sparked to life deep within her, burning hot and fierce. "Keep it, because wherever you go, wherever you stay...that's where I'll hang my hat."

"Oh, Holt," Cami whispered, and threw herself into his arms, nearly knocking him off his feet.

"Hey, watch it," he groused. "You're crushin' my hat."

"Here." She shoved his Stetson back into his hands. "The only place you'll be hanging this is at the A-OK Corral."

He nodded in satisfaction. "And I've got an extra bed knob for that silly pink one of yours, if you're interested."

Stricken, she bit her lip. "I...I don't have it any more."

A slow grin spread across his mouth. "You do now. I tied the fool thing to Loco's saddle. And let me tell you, he's none too happy about it." He cupped her face, his gaze growing serious...intent. "I love you, Cami. More than life itself. Will you marry me?"

"You folks staying or leaving?" the conductor demanded, practically dancing at Holt's elbow. "We've got a schedule to keep."

"Do it, Colorado. Marry him, Cami!" the passengers shouted.

"Yes," she said, with a smile that felt a mile wide. "Yes, I'll marry you. Let's go home. All right?"

Holt didn't say a word. He didn't have to. His expression said it all. Then he kissed her.

"We're late! We're late!" shrieked the conductor, throwing his schedule to the ground and stomping on it. "Make up your minds! Are you coming or going?"

Reluctantly Holt released her. "Going." And without further ado he swept Cami into his arms, luggage and all, and carried her from the train. As he strode across the platform, a dozen cars screeched to a halt and neighbors and townsfolk, guests and wranglers alike poured from the vehicles.

"He got her!" shouted Gabby. "He broke the record and got her!" Cheers erupted.

Cami buried her face in Holt's shirt. She was home at last. Lordy, it felt good.

"I did it, Daddy," she whispered. "I'm finally a cowboy. Just like you."

EPILOGUE

WITH SPRING CAME THE first wave of guests to the A-OK Corral and Cami sat in her rocker on the porch relaxing and enjoying the view while she waited.

A plume of dust appeared on the horizon, heralding the arrival of a vehicle. A few minutes later, a station wagon pulled into the yard and a man in his late thirties climbed from behind the wheel, looking around in bewilderment. He poked his head in the open car window and said something to the woman seated on the passenger side. In the back, Cami could see several wriggling children. The family's youngest member announced his presence with a strident wail.

Cami stood, hitched up her britches and strode over to the car. Behind her the ranch door slammed open and footsteps, remarkably similar to the sound made by a herd of elephants, clattered down the porch steps after her. Two black-haired urchins arrived breathless at her side.

"Howdy!" she called to the man over the shrieks of the baby. She stuck out her hand. "I'm Colorado Cami, C.C. for short. Where do you folks hail from? Ohio? That's all right." She gave them a mischievous wink. "We won't hold it against you. What do you say, we get you unloaded? My boys here, Flint and Colt, will help you with anything you need. And by the way...welcome to the A-OK Corral!"

Relive the romance...
Harlequin and Silhouette
are proud to present

A program of collections of three complete novels by the most-requested authors with the most-requested themes. Be sure to look for one volume each month with three complete novels by top-name authors.

In September: **BAD BOYS**   Dixie Browning
                                       Ann Major
                                       Ginna Gray
No heart is safe when these hot-blooded hunks are in town!

In October: **DREAMSCAPE**   Jayne Ann Krentz
                                         Anne Stuart
                                         Bobby Hutchinson
Something's happening! But is it love or magic?

In December: **SOLUTION: MARRIAGE**   Debbie Macomber
                                                  Annette Broadrick
                                                    Heather Graham Pozzessere
Marriages in name only have a way of leading to love....

Available at your favorite retail outlet.

REQ-G2

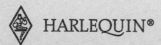

This Valentine's Day
give yourself something special. Something that's
just right for the most romantic day of the year.
Something that's all about love...

TWO FOR THE

HEART

Two brand-new stories in one volume!
THE PROPOSAL by Betty Neels,
a favorite author for almost twenty-five years
and
THE ENGAGEMENT by Ellen James,
a new author with a fast-growing readership
Two brand-new stories that will satisfy,
charm and delight you!

 HARLEQUIN ROMANCE®

From the heart and for the heart—
especially on Valentine's Day....
Available in February, wherever
Harlequin books are sold.

My Valentine
1994

Celebrate the most romantic day of the year with
MY VALENTINE 1994
a collection of original stories, written by
four of Harlequin's most popular authors...

**MARGOT DALTON
MURIEL JENSEN
MARISA CARROLL
KAREN YOUNG**

*Available in February, wherever
Harlequin Books are sold.*

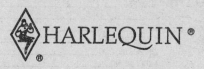

HARLEQUIN ®

VAL94

Harlequin Romance invites you...

BACK TO THE

As you enjoy your Harlequin Romance® BACK TO THE
RANCH stories each month, you can collect four proofs of
purchase to redeem for an attractive gold-toned charm bracelet
complete with five Western-themed charms. The bracelet will
make a unique addition to your jewelry collection or a
distinctive gift for that special someone.

One proof of purchase can be found in the back pages of each
BACK TO THE RANCH title...one every month until
May 1994.

To receive your gift, please fill out the information below and mail four (4) original proof-of-
purchase coupons from any Harlequin Romance **BACK TO THE RANCH** title plus $2.50 for
postage and handling (check or money order—do not send cash), payable to Harlequin Books,
to: **IN THE U.S.**: P.O. Box 9056, Buffalo, NY, 14269-9056; **IN CANADA**: P.O. Box 621, Fort
Erie, Ontario, L2A 5X3.

Requests must be received by June 30, 1994.

Please allow 4-6 weeks after receipt of order for delivery.

BACK TO THE RANCH

NAME: _____
ADDRESS: _____
_____
CITY: _____
STATE/PROVINCE: _____
ZIP/POSTAL CODE: _____
ACCOUNT NO.: _____

ONE PROOF OF PURCHASE   091 KAX